THE GUARDIAN'S CHOICE

CELTIC CURSES
BOOK THREE

L.M. HATCHELL

The Guardian's Choice

Celtic Curses (Book 3)

First published by ALX Publishing 2024

Cover Design by Atra Luna Book Cover Designs

Editing by Two Birds Author Services

Copyright © 2024 by L.M. Hatchell

This novel is entirely a work of fiction. The names, characters and incidents portrayed in it are the work of the author's imagination. Any resemblance to actual persons, living or dead, events or localities is entirely coincidental.

For the people willing to stand in times of darkness

CHAPTER ONE

I watched the last spark of life drain from the piercing black eyes. Watched the vitality and energy fade away to nothing. Shadows engulfed me. They wrapped around me, swirling faster and faster until my head swam and the world ceased to be.

My mouth opened on a scream, but no sound came out. The darkness consumed it as wholly as it consumed me. Drowning, I clawed my way for a surface I no longer believed existed.

There was no escape, no forgiveness. Just the truth of my actions and the stain left forever on my soul. This was my fate. And I deserved it.

With a flutter of my eyelids, the scene changed. I was in my bedroom in Teagan's apartment, and an all-consuming darkness filled the space. At the end of my bed, a shadowy figure loomed.

This time when a scream bubbled up in my throat,

shadows wrapped around my neck and cut the sound off before it could emerge. Panic filled every fibre of my being, and everything went black.

I deserved this.

There was the distant sound of my name being called, and then a sharp bang. My eyes snapped open and I jerked upright with a gasped inhale.

I was still in my room, but now light filtered in around the edges of my curtain, chasing away any remnants of night. No shadowy figure stood at the end of the bed, though my heart refused to believe what my eyes were telling me as it thundered in my chest.

The bang sounded again, and I belatedly realised when Teagan's impatient call came that she was knocking on the door to wake me.

"Come on, Aisling. Get your butt out of bed. We need to get going."

I blinked, scanning the room again in case I'd somehow missed the looming threat that had been present only moments ago in my mind. Had it all been a dream? With trembling fingers, I reached up to touch my throat. It had seemed so real. *He* had seemed so real.

"Aisling!"

Giving myself a mental and physical shake, I focused on the irritation clear in Teagan's tone to bring me back to reality. I'd avoided accompanying Teagan to her training sessions for the past couple of weeks, and her patience was wearing thin with my excuses. I'd made a promise to support her and I needed to keep it.

Besides, the alternative was to stay at home alone.

"I'm coming," I called hoarsely as I swung my legs out from under the covers.

I reached down for my trusty unicorn slippers and frowned when I couldn't find them next to the bed where I always left them. Unease slithered through me as I cast my eyes around the empty bedroom.

There at the end of the bed were my slippers, waiting patiently for me. As if they'd always been there.

The sterile white room formed a sharp contrast to Teagan's raven hair. Padded walls surrounded her on three sides, and as I watched her from the far side of the viewing window, I couldn't help but glance again at the open door to reassure myself she could leave whenever she wanted.

Men and women in white coats buzzed around the small observation room where I stood fidgeting uncomfortably. They paid me no heed as they analysed graphs on their computer screens and talked in acronyms that made zero sense to me. I was little more than a human-shaped obstacle to be walked around as they prepared for the next experiment.

An auburn-haired woman leaned forward and pressed a button on the keyboard in front of her. "We're ready to go if you are, Teagan?"

Maggie, I'd been told, was leading the research team helping Teagan explore and "train" her newfound banshee nature. Her hard features and overall lack of warmth hadn't endeared me to her when we were introduced, but Teagan seemed fond of her. And that was why I was here, wasn't it – for Teagan? It sure as hell wasn't because I wanted to play nice with the Watchers.

Teagan seemed to hesitate for a moment before turning to give Maggie a thumbs up. Her eyes sought me out and I attempted an encouraging smile, but if the uncertainty in my friend's expression was anything to go by, I failed.

With a hiss, the door to the white room closed, sealing tight. A wiry man with thick–rimmed glasses appeared in front of me, startling me. He held out a pair of padded headphones. "Don't take these off until Maggie gives the signal."

I nodded mutely and put them on.

The shift was instantaneous and disorientating. All sound disappeared, and it was like I'd suddenly found myself in a silent movie. Around me, the team all donned similar headphones and settled themselves into position in front of the various screens, ready to begin.

Aside from Teagan herself, I was the only person here who had had the pleasure of experiencing Teagan's banshee scream up close and personal without any protective equipment. Memory of the excruciating agony was enough to make my palms leak sweat now, even knowing both the room and protective equipment were soundproof.

A disembodied voice came through the headphones. "Okay, Teagan. Whenever you're ready."

Butterflies did an uneasy jig in my stomach as Teagan gave a shallow nod. Her ribs expanded as she took a deep breath. Then she screamed.

I flinched and jerked my hands up to hold my headphones in place as the sound screeched across my nerves and raked down my spine. It permeated my very soul and sent a wave of primal terror through me.

The team around me showed similar signs of discomfort, with many of them grimacing in pain, and some even gripping the desk in front of them with white knuckles. None of them appeared to be surprised by the reaction, however.

Graphs flared to life on the computer screens, and red errors flashed up as lines surpassed peak values.

It took me a moment before I realised the screaming had stopped. My whole body trembled, and I had to dig my nails into the palms of my hands to ground myself again. *Well, that was interesting.*

Maggie pointed to my headphones and gave me a thumbs up to indicate it was safe to remove them. Call me overcautious, but I waited until she and a number of others on her team had removed theirs before I followed suit. I looked from the group of white coats, now huddled around screens and talking excitedly amongst themselves, to the sterile room where Teagan stood, unmoving.

"I thought you said the room was fully soundproof?" I didn't even try to keep the accusation from my voice. My nerves were still raw, and I had to stop myself from checking that my brains were where they should be and not leaking out my nose or ears.

Maggie looked up from the graph she was examining, her eyes feverish with excitement. "It is."

The surety in her statement sent a shiver of unease running through me.

Before I could think any more on it, the door to the white room hissed open and Teagan stepped out. She scanned the observation room until her eyes fell on me. The uncertainty in her expression made my heart clench.

I pasted a smile on my face and walked over to her. "I see the vocal lessons have paid off."

She let out a surprised laugh, and some of the tension eased from her shoulders. "My range has definitely expanded."

Maggie appeared at her side, clipboard in hand. "That it has. Your readings are off the charts today. How are you feeling?"

Teagan brushed her dark hair back from her face. "Good. Strong."

Maggie nodded, as if that was the answer she expected, and I couldn't help the irritation that caused me to clench my teeth. Teagan was a person, not a maths equation. The Watchers might have agreed to help her figure out her new nature, but I couldn't shake the feeling that this whole thing was some kind of messed-up science experiment. I bit my lip and forced myself to stay quiet.

"I'd like to try something new." Maggie tapped her clipboard with her pen. "If you're up for it, of course?"

Teagan's expression turned wary, and I could've sworn she was carefully avoiding my gaze. "What do I need to do?"

The smile Maggie gave her did nothing to conceal the calculating gleam in the woman's eyes. "There's only so much computers can tell us about your powers," Maggie explained in a tone so reasonable that I instantly tensed.

"Already with your progression in the last couple of weeks your readings are off the charts. Given the nature of your talent, it's difficult to run a live test. But we'd like to at least establish a baseline. We'll use a rat from the lab. Nothing big, of course."

Teagan blanched, her naturally pale features turning a sickly green that matched my own reaction.

I gaped at Maggie. "Surely you're not suggesting that she try scream a rat to death?"

Maggie's smile cooled noticeably as she turned her attention to me. "Based on what Teagan has told us of her past experiences and on the readings here today, it is the most likely outcome, yes. While I understand it might seem distasteful to you, Teagan's power poses a great danger to those around her. It is important that we establish a baseline so that we can map out our next steps in helping her."

I saw red, and all my best intentions to bite my tongue were forgotten in an instant. "Helping her? Turning her into a weapon you mean."

The last vestige of feigned friendliness dropped as her expression hardened. "I'm not sure exactly what it is you think we do here, Ms. O'Meara, but I shall leave you two alone for a few minutes so that *Teagan* can decide how she would like to proceed."

The emphasis was punctuated by a kind smile for Teagan and a reassuring squeeze of the shoulder before Maggie returned to her team.

I searched my friend's face for the disgust that I was sure would match my own. Teagan refused to even squash a spider; there was no way she'd do something this cruel.

But the disgust I expected to see wasn't there. Only a grim acceptance.

"You're not actually considering this, are you?" I demanded.

Teagan refused to meet my eyes as she shrugged. "It's just a rat. It's going to die in the lab anyway."

"You can't be serious."

She straightened, her jaw tightening as she whirled on me. "What do you expect me to do, Aisling? Find out the hard way where the line is when I kill someone?"

I reared back, her words like a physical slap. She knew how much the two deaths I was responsible for haunted me, knew I'd give anything to take them back – even if Dothar and Dain had been evil psychopaths. Her comment may have come from a place of fear about her own abilities, but I couldn't help the hurt that tightened my chest.

Realising what she'd said, Teagan seemed to deflate, her shoulders slumping. "I need to do this. It's the only way."

With that, she turned and gave Maggie a nod, then strode back into the white room.

Sick to my stomach, I turned my back on the sterile white room. This was all my fault. It was the magic I brought back that had caused Teagan's dormant banshee genetics to be activated. I was the reason she was standing in there right this minute, ready to kill a defenceless creature just to convince herself she still had some semblance of control over her life.

I stumbled out of the observation room, desperate to put as much space between the white room and myself as possible. Not sure exactly where I was going, I followed the winding grey corridor back to the training centre that formed the heart of the Watchers of Danu headquarters. Teagan had driven us here to make sure I didn't find another excuse to avoid coming. That meant I couldn't leave now. But I had no intention of leaving without her anyway; I just needed space.

The corridor ascended at an almost imperceptible

climb, and as I covered more distance, the air seemed to grow lighter, less cloying. A loud crash of weights hitting the floor told me I'd reached the training centre even before I came to an open door on my left. Not wanting to seem like I was snooping, I tried to appear casual as I glanced inside the room.

Mirrors lined the wall opposite the doorway, and racks of weights and benches filled the space. A brawny man with a buzz cut was the gym's sole occupant. A barbell lay discarded at his feet, and though I didn't know a lot about weight-lifting, I couldn't help but notice that the plates on either end of the bar were big and that there was a hell of a lot of them. Catching sight of me in the mirror, the man stood and stared at me, unblinking.

Uncomfortable, I hurried on.

The next rooms I passed appeared to be geared towards various types of rehabilitation. One door listed a range of heat treatments available inside, including infrared and saunas. While the next one down listed a range of cold treatments, including ice baths and a plunge pool. I shivered at the thought.

I knew from the time I spent here after my near-death experience at the hands of the sons of Carmen that the hospital wing was close by. I hadn't exactly been in the right frame of mind at that time to appreciate the sheer scale of the place, but now I couldn't help wondering why the Watchers needed all of these facilities.

The reminder of that day had me looking around

and eyeing any mere hint of a shadow warily. For two weeks I'd waited for Dub to appear, to step out of a shadow and exact revenge for his brothers' deaths. Aside from a nightly appearance in my dreams, there had been no sign of him.

Since he hadn't struck me as the waiting-patiently type – and my sanity was hanging on tenterhooks – I'd started telling myself he actually died that night alongside his brothers. No one had seen him escape, so it could be true. Of course, saying that and believing it were two different things, and being here again was messing with my head.

I blew out a shaky breath and veered right, away from the hospital wing and the bad memories.

Before long, I came to a set of open double doors that revealed a large hall. Goals were set up at either end, and a group of men and women were playing indoor soccer. A slide tackle from one of the men caused shouts of protest, while one of the women took advantage of the distraction to kick the ball into the goal nearest me. Good-natured taunts filled the space, and I was pretty sure I caught a reference to the goalie's mother thrown in.

I was about to continue on my way when a skinny red-headed man turned and spotted me. "Oh look, the great and powerful Guardian has graced us with her presence. Should we bow?"

My cheeks flared with heat as they all turned to look. Some of the gazes that fixed on me were curious, but others were downright hostile. Mr. Big Balls fell firmly into the second category. Not really sure how to respond – *Yes, please bow before my greatness?* – I turned to leave.

"That's right," he called. "Run away. You're good at that, aren't you?"

I stopped, anger flaring in me. What the hell did this man know about me?

Before I could utter the retort poised on the tip of my tongue, a woman with salt-and-pepper hair picked up the ball and threw it at him. "Stop being a knob, Richie. We have a game to finish."

I took the interruption as my cue to leave, and turned to hurry down back down the corridor. Richie wasn't the first Watcher I'd met this morning who made it clear I was far from their favourite person. The unfairness of it stung. No, I couldn't control what people thought of me, but I couldn't control my ancestry either. I'd never asked to be the Guardian.

The backs of my eyes burned and I clenched my teeth, refusing to let their judgement get the best of me. I turned a corner and slammed straight into my ex-boyfriend.

I stumbled back, blinking in surprise.

Pete dropped his training bag and reached out to steady me. "Hey. I didn't expect to see you here."

His warm brown eyes assessed me with an all too knowing look, and I gave him a weak smile. "I ran out of excuses."

Trying not to be too obvious about it, I scanned him from head to toe. His black hair was still wet from a shower and flopped in its usual unkempt mess around his face. Colour had finally started returning to his cheeks, and he'd lost some of the cornered animal look that I'd worried might become a permanent feature.

When Pete's werewolf genetics had kicked in, he'd isolated himself from his friends and family, terrified of what was happening to him. Being forcibly kept from his wolf by the sons of Carmen had had the unexpected side effect of helping him accept his animal side. It had taken him time to recover from the effects of the separation and the silver, but I was relieved to see him standing taller, no longer slumped into himself, hiding.

"I didn't realise you'd be here today, or I'd have popped in to see how you were," I said, suddenly uncomfortable with the silence between us. "How's the rehab going?"

He ran his hand through his damp hair, and this time it was his smile that was weary. "I'm getting there. It's taking time to get my strength back, but it's a big help having access to the facilities here. I can let my wolf free without the worry that..."

The worry that someone would try to permanently separate them again.

I reached out to squeeze his arm but dropped my hand. It had been a few months since I ended our three-year relationship. I still cared for him a great deal, but I wasn't sure if it was my place to be the one offering him comfort anymore. The last thing I wanted to do was give him mixed signals.

"But your wolf's okay? You're okay?" I asked, unable to completely ignore the need to reassure myself.

"We're getting used to each other." He shoved his hands into the pockets of his jeans and looked at the ground. "It's frustrating not knowing quite what will trigger a shift and leave me lying somewhere unconscious. My control is getting better though. And at least here I'm not defenceless."

I thought back to the day I'd accidentally stumbled over Pete's unconscious body in the Phoenix Park. His wolf had sensed the danger of Dub's presence, and it had triggered the shift. The whole thing had been a huge shock for me so I couldn't even begin to imagine what it was like to be him. An all too familiar guilt twisted my insides.

"It's hard for her too, you know."

I blinked, confused at the change in conversation while I'd been lost in thought.

"Teagan." Pete clarified. "I know you don't like her training with the Watchers, but you're not in her shoes. You need to let her figure this out in her own way."

Shame heated my cheeks at his soft chastisement, and he gave me a sympathetic smile.

"We're all just muddling our way through this as best we can. You two will figure it out." He picked up his training bag from where he'd dropped it. "Give me a call if you need anything."

I gave him a distracted wave as he headed for a lift at the end of the corridor. As the doors slid shut behind him, I considered his words.

My own introduction to magic hadn't exactly been smooth sailing. Teagan had to bear the burden of knowing when a person was going to die, and she didn't even have the benefit of a magical dream tutor to help her. Would I have handled things as well as she had in her shoes? Not if my track record was anything to go by. The last thing she needed was me making things even harder.

Resolved to make up for my shaky at best support, I turned and headed back to the testing lab where her training session was being held. As I neared the observation room, I hesitated.

Was it safe for me to go in?

Surely they'd have to put signs up or something if they were in the middle of a test that required protective equipment.

Nervously, I edged closer.

When my ears didn't start to bleed, I relaxed marginally. Only the sound of hushed conversations drifted from the room so I stepped inside, only to draw up short.

Maggie stood on the far side of the room speaking quietly to a stocky bald man. Brian – my least favourite of the Watchers – frowned at whatever she was saying. He turned his gaze to the white room where Teagan stood alone, and his frown deepened.

Curious, and more than a little suspicious, I edged further into the room, trying not to draw their attention. Clearly I'd failed "stealth spying 101" however, as my foot struck the corner of the computer desk. I let a hiss of pain.

All eyes in the room turned to me, and Brian scowled as he became aware of my presence. Without another word, he stalked from the room, leaving me alone with Maggie and the team.

I debated demanding answers from Maggie about what she and Brian were discussing, but the door to the white room opened and Teagan stepped out. Her eyes fell on me and she hesitated, uncertain.

"I didn't know if you'd left."

Remembering Pete's words and my recent resolution, I pushed away my suspicions and gave my friend what I hoped was a relaxed smile. "Nope. Just getting my step count in for the day."

CHAPTER THREE

The familiar meadow of the dreamscape took form around me. As always, lush green grass cushioned me where I sat, and the sun warmed my bare arms. In the distance, I could hear birds chirping, but other than that, I was alone.

I inhaled deeply, waiting for a sense of calm to wash over me like it normally did. I was left waiting. Tonight, it seemed, the worries that plagued my waking thoughts were determined to follow me even into sleep.

Memories of Maggie and Brian's conversation nagged at me. I'd tried to broach the subject with Teagan in the car on our way home, but she'd shrugged it off. She suggested that Brian might simply have been enquiring about her progress and had even pointed out that it wasn't unusual for two colleagues to talk. The not-so-subtle inference was of course that my mistrust of the Watchers was making me read more into the situation than there was.

It was a fair point that I couldn't really argue. Still, the niggling sense that I'd missed something important about the interaction stayed with me.

Teagan hadn't seemed herself after leaving the Watchers' HQ either. Aside from the brief debate regarding Brian and Maggie's questionable intentions, she'd been oddly silent for most of the drive. I wasn't sure if she was waiting for me to ask about the rat, but I couldn't do it. As soon as we got back to the apartment, she'd excused herself with a migraine and gone to bed.

I sighed in frustration and tilted my face up to let the heat of the sun bathe my skin. Maybe I could just stay here? Things were so much simpler in the dreamscape. Yes, Killian tortured me nightly with magic drills and quizzes, but now that I was getting a better grasp on my connection to magic, they were actually kind of fun.

Plus, if I was here, Killian wouldn't have to be alone so much.

As if summoned by my thoughts, my magical dream tutor emerged from the trees on my right-hand side. He wore his usual faded jeans and white t-shirt with an unbuttoned black shirt over it. His jaw-length light brown hair was pulled back from his face, and as he approached, I mused on the fact that it never seemed to grow any longer.

Did anything ever change for him here in this place? Or was he for all intents and purposes still held in that millennia-long stasis, alive only when it was time to do his duty as my mentor? The thought hurt my heart.

"If you keep frowning like that, you're going to give yourself wrinkles," he said, dropping to the ground next to me and draping his arms over his bent knees. "Not something you can afford at your age."

I swatted his arm and mock glared at him. "Hey! I'll have you know I look very young for thirty."

A raised eyebrow was his only response, but I could've sworn I saw the corner of his lip twitch.

Pushing away my morose wonderings about his existence, I shifted my attention to the trees on the horizon. "I went with Teagan to the Watchers' head-quarters."

"You finally gave in?"

"Yeah. She wasn't saying it, but I could see she was hurt I hadn't been to her training. I didn't want her to think I have a problem with her being a banshee."

"Do you?"

I glanced at him in surprise. "No. I have a problem with the Watchers using her for their own ends."

"How do you think they're using her?"

Remembering the small white rat being carried into the sterile testing room, I shivered. For some reason, I didn't want to tell Killian about the live test. It wasn't that I thought he'd judge Teagan – he always seemed to be able to look at things in a level-headed manner – but if I said it out loud, I'd have to admit to myself that maybe *I* was judging her.

"I don't know," I said instead, not quite meeting his dark eyes that saw too much. "The whole thing just seemed very cold and clinical, like she was a test subject to be studied rather than a person they were trying to help."

I didn't miss the almost imperceptible tightening in Killian's expression as he considered my words. He seemed unsettled by what I said, and for once, he didn't automatically put forward an argument in defence of the Watchers.

Tentatively, I voiced the real concern that had been repeating over and over in my head. "How do we know they're the good guys?"

Killian shifted his body to face me with his full attention, and I couldn't help but notice the ripple of muscle beneath his t-shirt.

"What do you mean?"

"Well, we know the Order of the Fomori are in the bad guys category. If that hadn't been clear enough by the whole trick-me-into-releasing-magic thing, then contracting the sons of Carmen pretty much sealed the deal."

Even mentioning the three brothers made my stomach clench in instinctual panic. Of course, we couldn't be sure that the Order had requested the brothers commit the sacrificial killings on their behalf. But the brothers had indicated as much during the fun little escapade when they tried to use me as one of the victims.

"My point is," I continued once my racing heart

calmed to a more respectable level of panic. "Just because the Order are bad doesn't make the Watchers the good guys by default. What do we really know about them? Yes, we share some of the same bloodline connections, but I'm sure plenty of the Tuatha were dicks too. Just because we all evolved from them doesn't mean our moral leanings are set in stone."

Shadows darkened Killian's eyes, and I silently cursed my insensitivity. Too often, I forgot that Killian was one of the original Tuatha. One of the people who had sacrificed their whole lives to keep magic, and the rest of us, safe. Yes, it was likely that some of them were dicks regardless of that fact, but it didn't mean I had to be so irreverent in bringing them into this.

Time for a swift change of subject before I depressed us both.

Giving Killian a playful nudge with my shoulder, I asked, "What cruel and unusual punishment do you have in store for me today, boss?"

He glanced sideways at me, and the glint of amusement chased the shadows from his eyes. My stomach did a little flippity-flop.

Rising to his feet, he held out a hand. I hesitated a moment before taking it. The warmth of his touch seeped into me, and I was reminded just how solid and real he was – here in this dreamscape, at least.

"I want to work on something a little different today," he said once I was standing.

Something about his tone caused me to take a wary step back.

For the past few weeks, I'd been learning how to recognise and tap into the magic around me. We'd been building up a repertoire of basic skills, and I'd gotten pretty good at using external energy to enhance my own physical processes – heating up and cooling down my body, generating short bursts of increased speed, temporarily enhancing the force my muscles could generate. I knew these things by no means made me an expert and there was still a lot to learn, but I suddenly wasn't feeling so eager about that learning.

Killian watched me as if he expected me to bolt at any second. "You're right," he said. "We don't truly know anything about the Watchers or their intentions. And I fear it won't be long before the Order regroup. We need to make sure you're in the best position to protect yourself. So, it's time we start developing your innate gifts."

I frowned, confused. "Innate gifts?"

He nodded. "All magic users show a preference towards certain types of use, but some bloodlines carry an affinity for more ... unique forms of magic that aren't accessible to others. At least not without compli- cated rituals or the assistance of rare magical artefacts."

"And I come from one of those bloodlines?"

He nodded again.

From some of the things Killian had told me in the past, I'd already gathered that my ancestors ranked high within the power structure of the original Tuatha Dé Danann. I hadn't given much thought as to what that might mean, but I guess it stood to reason that only powerful magic users would hold the most powerful positions.

"Do Teagan and Pete fall into this category too?" I asked, partly out of curiosity, partly to delay asking more about my own bloodline.

"Yes. Their gifts are the foundations for some of these talents. Pete's shifting is the original starting point for a type of magic we now know as Whispering. It's an ability to speak with, and in some really rare cases that are closest to the origin bloodline, control animals. The Seer ability – a form of premonition – is a watered-down continuation of the banshee's death foresight."

"What about you? You said you're a Dreamwalker, right? Is that one of these talents?"

Once more those shadows darkened Killian's brown eyes, and I wished I could take the question back. "It's one of the rarer ones, and the reason I was most suited for this role," he answered, his tone giving away nothing of his feelings on the matter.

I wasn't fooled, though. I knew what it was like to be thrust into a role purely because of a genetic situation you had no choice in. For him to have to resign himself to a lifetime in limbo... Surely, no one could have expected that from him, genetic suitability or not?

"We've touched a bit on Elemental magic in the drills we've been working on. It's not your strongest ability, but it typically runs through the general Tuatha line in some form or other. The strongest Elementals can use that magic on a much larger scale and can manipulate the environment around them as well as themselves."

"Okay." I swallowed, my mouth suddenly dry. "If that's not my strongest ability, what is?"

His pause sent butterflies careening around my stomach, and I had to bite my tongue to stop myself from yelling at him to just spit it out.

"Siphoning."

At first the word didn't make any sense to me. I frowned, trying to understand what he meant. Then it clicked.

"You mean..." The words left my mouth in a horrified whisper as the realisation of what he was saying settled over me. "You mean draining someone like I did when I killed Dothar and Dain."

He gave me a sympathetic look, but it didn't change the determined expression on his face. We were doing this, no matter how uncomfortable it made me.

"What happened with the brothers was different," he said. "You had no training, and it was a life-or-death situation. If your instincts hadn't driven you to reach for your siphoning powers, you would be the one dead now, not them."

He was right. Logically, I knew that. It was even likely that many others would have died too if the brothers had survived to gather more power. But it didn't stop the guilt haunting my every waking minute, or the nightmares that waited in the moments of sleep before the dreamscape formed. And it didn't stop me from wondering what it said about me that I was glad they were both dead.

"Try not to think about siphoning as draining life force, but rather as a way to disable an opponent's greatest weapon – their magic. Once you master it, you won't have to worry about going too far. But if you don't train the gift, you'll be forever at its mercy."

I chewed on my lip, considering that. The last thing I wanted was to live in constant fear of killing someone. Still, I hesitated.

Killian reached out a hand and brushed something wet from my cheek. When had I started crying?

"I believe in you, Aisling." He held my gaze, nothing but sincerity in his eyes. "Trust me."

I sucked in a breath. And reached for his hand.

CHAPTER FOUR

Bright light seared my eyelids and I cringed away from it, huddling deeper into the protection of my warm blankets. I wasn't ready to wake up and face the world yet.

Memories of the night's training session flashed through my mind. Killian's warm hand. His trusting eyes. The terror that I might hurt him when he insisted on acting as the guinea pig for our session.

We'd only scratched the surface of my siphoning ability, examining the tethers that connected me to another's magic and would allow me to pull that magic to me if I so wished. I didn't wish. I couldn't think of anything more horrid than this power that was my so-called innate gift. To be so easily able to take the life force of another? It was barbaric. I shuddered despite the warmth that cocooned me.

That wasn't to say I was blind to the protection the gift afforded me, or that I didn't understand why

Killian wanted me to practice using it. I needed to learn how to control it, or I ran the risk of hurting somebody else – just like Teagan and her banshee gift.

The parallel with my friend's situation all but jumped up and smacked me in the forehead. I was such a bloody idiot. How had I not seen it sooner?

I'd been saying I understood how hard it was for her and that I wanted to support her, but had I truly tried my hardest? I had Killian to help guide me through all this magic stuff, and yet I'd subconsciously judged her for turning to the Watchers for help just because I didn't like them. Ugh, I was a crappy friend.

Well, that ended today.

Shoving the covers off me, I swung my legs over the side of the bed and slid my feet into my unicorn slippers. I found Teagan in the kitchen, her head all but buried in the worn leather satchel she used for work.

"Let's do brunch," I blurted, perhaps a tad too enthusiastically.

Apparently not having noticed my appearance, Teagan jumped a mile. She swore, clutching her bag to her with a scowl.

"Dammit, Aisling. I'm going to get you a bell. You nearly gave me a heart attack."

I blinked, taken aback by her irritated tone. Maybe she hadn't slept well because of the migraine?

"What do you say?" I asked, a little more tentatively this time. "You, me, bottomless brunch cocktails? It's been too long since we had some fun."

Teagan looked down at her bag, and I could've

sworn there was guilt written across her face as she hesitated. When she looked back up, both the irritation and any guilt I might have imagined were gone. Her expression was shuttered and she didn't quite meet my eyes.

"Sorry." She reached for the car keys that lay on the table next to her bag. "I need to be somewhere. Research project for work."

A research project? She hadn't mentioned that she was working on anything new. My heart sank.

Normally Teagan couldn't wait to burn the ears off me about a new project that had piqued her attention. Had things gotten so bad between us that she didn't feel like she could share the details of her normal life with me anymore? Or was I just being oversensitive?

I tried not to let the disappointment show on my face. "Oh, okay. No problem. Maybe we can do it next weekend instead?"

Teagan didn't seem to hear me as she gave her bag a final check before shouldering it.

"Where is the exotic world of academic research taking you today?" I tried again as she reached for her coat.

I waited to see the spark of excitement in her eyes when she realised she hadn't yet regaled me with the details. It didn't come. In fact, she didn't even seem to have heard my question as she headed for the door. She reached for the door handle and paused, turning back to me. For a moment, hope surged in me.

"I almost forgot, Brian wants to talk to you about a job offer. He's going to call you this morning."

My thoughts stuttered to a stop, and I stared at her. "What?"

"I told him you were looking for something a bit more permanent since leaving Smith & Mercer, and he said the Watchers had an opening that would be perfect for you." She gave me a beseeching look. "I have to go, but promise me you'll at least hear him out."

I opened my mouth, ready to declare in no uncertain terms that I'd be working for the Watchers over my dead body. But I snapped it shut again.

Teagan had graciously offered up her spare bedroom when I moved out of the house I'd rented with Pete. She'd saved me from having to move home to my mam's – its own kind of torture – and hadn't once complained about the fact I was still here. In return, I made it my business to pay my part of the rent on time and be as easy a housemate to live with as possible.

Since recent events had made it untenable for me to go back to my job at Smith & Mercer – them representing the people who had tried to kill me and all that – I'd been taking temp jobs to keep on top of things. Thankfully, my finances hadn't taken a hit just yet, but it was by no means stable employment, which pretty much put the kibosh on any mortgage applications. Could I really say no without a viable alternative to offer up?

I felt the Watchers dig their metaphorical claws

deeper into my flesh as I nodded wordlessly and glared at the floor. The door closed with a soft click as Teagan left.

Alone with only the silence of the apartment and my simmering irritation, I was at a loss for what to do with myself. Since it didn't look like brunch was on the cards, I slumped over to the kitchen and pulled a random box of cereal out of the press. A bowl, a splash of milk, and a spoon later and I curled up on the sofa with the sugary goodness.

Every spoonful I put into my mouth tasted like sawdust.

When had this void developed between me and Teagan? I knew we didn't see eye to eye when it came to the Watchers, but had things really gotten this bad in our friendship? Ever since we were teenagers, we'd been inseparable. I refused to believe that a small difference of opinion could drive a wedge between us now.

Feeling maudlin and in need of a distraction, I did what all healthy adults did – picked up my phone and started doomscrolling. I'd developed the bad habit after the events at the Church of the Blessed Heart a couple of weeks ago. Brian had assured me that the Watchers had dealt with any evidence I, my friends, or the sons of Carmen has been there that night. Still, I couldn't help myself from scanning news reports for any mention of the dead bodies or a warrant for my arrest.

In truth, I'd also hoped to find something that

would tell me for sure whether or not Dub lived. The Watchers had found no trace of the brother who walked in shadow, and my memories were hazy at best. But my gut told me he was alive. So, why hadn't he come for me?

With that question just one of the many that continued to torment me, I idly scanned the news headlines.

Car crash kills three people.

Looming threat of nuclear war as political unrest continues.

Ancient disease destroys crops along east coast of Ireland.

Frowning, I stopped scrolling and clicked on the last headline. Ever since discovering my heritage and the existence of magic, I'd developed a healthy distrust of anything "ancient." While I couldn't quite see what my screw-up had to do with some strange disease, I still scanned the article warily.

A spate of unexplained crop deaths has left farmers along the east coast of Ireland fearing for their livelihoods. Scientists have yet to identify the cause of the mass crop failure, but early examinations suggest the soil contained traces of an organism that hasn't been seen in this part of the world for centuries.

Well, that was nice and vague. Curious, I did a quick online search to see if I could find anything more specific. Only two reports popped up among a spattering of unrelated stories.

That was strange.

It wasn't exactly unusual for news reports to overexaggerate, but if the situation was as bad as the first article suggested, shouldn't the farmers be up in arms? Clicking into the next link, I opened an article in the Agricultural Chronicles dated a few days previous.

The contamination was first identified in a small farm in Co. Wexford. While it is unknown at this point how the pathogen is moving, the spread appears to be forming a linear pattern, moving northwards from that point, with no sign of stopping.

A little of the tension in me released. Wexford was nowhere near the ritual site where I'd released magic; the chances of the two things being connected was slim at best. I was getting far too paranoid.

Grateful for one less thing to feel guilty about, I decided to treat myself to a spot of online shopping. Before I had a chance to finish typing my favourite store into the search bar, my phone buzzed. I scowled as a message from Brian appeared on the screen.

Meet me at HQ in an hour. Don't be late.

CHAPTER FIVE

A glance at the clock on my dashboard told me I was three minutes early as the barrier raised and I drove up the winding road to the Watchers of Danu headquarters. The grey industrial building loomed dead ahead, looking like it would be perfectly at home housing a large pharmaceutical company – which felt uncomfortably close to the truth given what I'd seen last time I was here.

I parked the car and climbed out, releasing a long, slow breath. *You promised Teagan you'd at least hear him out*, I reminded myself.

Squaring my shoulders, I crunched up the gravel path to the double glass doors that led to the reception. My hand had only just landed on the door handle when Brian appeared on the other side, his usual scowl fixed in place.

"You're on time," he said, pulling the door open.

I bit back my retort at the obvious disbelief in his

tone and pasted my sweetest smile on my face. "I'm nothing if not punctual."

He grunted and turned without a word, clearly expecting me to follow.

Already irritated by his attitude, I made rude gestures at him in my head. Outwardly, I of course kept my polite veneer in place and even gave the stony-faced receptionist a friendly wave as she tracked my every movement.

Brian led me to a door next to the reception and typed something into the keypad on the wall, being sure to block his movements from my view. There was a soft click, and the door opened to reveal a long corridor that led into the heart of the building. My previous visits to the HQ had been confined to the hospital wing and training centre, both located two storeys below ground. Now, I openly scanned my surroundings with curiosity.

Office doors lined either side of the corridor, each with small nameplates to indicate the occupant. At the end of the corridor, we passed a canteen and continued on through a large, open-plan office. At least twenty people sat at computer stations around the room, with many more desks sitting vacant.

"What do you guys actually do here?" I asked, suddenly realising I had no clue.

My initial introduction to the Watchers had been through Brian and his now-deceased partner, Siobhán. They'd both been Gardaí, and because of that I'd just assumed all the Watchers worked elsewhere and came together for weekly club meetings or something.

"Work."

I ground to a halt and crossed my arms. If he thought I was going to follow him around like a lapdog for sketchy, vague answers, he could take a run and jump. I had better things to do with my time – kind of.

Suddenly realising I'd stopped, Brian turned to look back. His scowl deepened, but he gave a relenting sigh. "The office staff here act as a central support hub for the Watchers. It's kind of like a one-stop shop where they can come for advice on education, finance, legal matters. Whatever they need."

"How do you fund it all?" He was making it sound like a quaint little citizen's advice office, but I'd seen the scale of the building and the type of facilities they had available on the lower levels.

"We have a number of members who are highly skilled in managing investments. For the most part we are self-sustaining, but we do have some families within the organisation who act as patrons to ensure any additional funding needs are met."

I raised an eyebrow, surprised at the relatively open response. It didn't exactly tell me all their deep, dark secrets, but it was more than I'd expected to get.

On the far side of the open-plan office, Brian keyed a code into yet another pin pad and led me down the next corridor. He stopped outside a closed door that showed his name in neat print on the small sign.

"Wait here," he ordered.

I snapped a mock salute at his back as he unlocked the door and stepped into what looked like a compulsively tidy office. Not bothering to hide my curiosity, I craned my neck to try get a better view through the narrow opening he'd left. Before I could see anything of interest, he returned with a blank manilla folder in hand.

He glowered and beckoned for me to follow him.

The meeting room we made our way to was similar to many of the boardrooms I frequented in my former role as paralegal. The reminder of why I was here caused me to tense, and I sat down stiffly in the black leather chair Brian gestured to.

"What did Teagan tell you about why I wanted to meet you this morning?" Brian shuffled some pages within the manilla folder, not bothering to even look at me.

I bristled. Who trained this guy on HR? "She said you wanted to discuss a possible job with me. I promised her I'd hear you out."

The implied "otherwise I wouldn't be here" went unsaid, but Brian finally looked up and inclined his head in acknowledgement nonetheless. He took the pages from the folder and spread them across the table in front of me so I could see them clearly.

The pages contained photocopies of various newspaper articles that had been arranged into the most organised collage presentation I'd ever seen. A cursory scan showed me that all the headlines indicated some degree of magical context to the stories.

Ancient oak tree reappears overnight after having been cut down more than 100 years before.

Unexplained lights spotted over the moors with residents swearing they heard howling.

Cattle refuse to enter crop circle in local farm.

I scanned them, disconcerted by the possible suggestion of magic but confused as to what they had to do with this job interview. My assumption when Teagan said Brian wanted to talk to me about a job was that it would be something law-related. I had also considered the magic avenue, though I guessed it would be something along the lines of donning a lab rat costume and letting their scientists poke around my insides.

"We've been monitoring media channels closely since the solstice," Brian explained, apparently noting my confusion. "So far, the signs that magic has returned have been minor enough, and nobody seems to be taking them seriously. But it's only a matter of time before the magic grows stronger and that changes. I don't need to tell you what will happen then."

Widespread panic and some good old cathartic burning at the stake if history was anything to go by.

I swallowed hard. "Okay. So, what has it got to do with me being here now?"

Brian leaned back in his chair and assessed me for a long moment. "We want you to head up a PR team that will be responsible for managing the situation."

Say what?

"So far we've been able to keep anything significant

from leaking to the press. Silly little tabloid articles like these aside." He gestured to the printouts that lay on the desk between us. "But we're already seeing magical abilities emerge with many of the Watchers, so it only stands to reason that it's happening elsewhere too. We're working to trace ancestral lines so that we might intercept these cases before they accidentally draw attention to themselves. Your job would be to make sure nothing slips through the net."

"How exactly would I do that?"

"Use your charms."

I almost laughed at his deadpan expression. We both knew he didn't think I had any charm worth speaking of. The only logical explanation for why he would pretend otherwise was if he wanted my face to be at the forefront of any fallout.

"You want me to be a scapegoat if everything goes to shit," I said, my tone remarkably calm all things considered.

Brian's expression hardened. "I *want* you to take responsibility for the mess *you* caused. If you hadn't released magic, we wouldn't be in this situation. The Watchers are keeping it contained as best we can, but you need to do your part."

I scrubbed a hand over my face, trying to get my thoughts straight. He wasn't wrong – this whole mess had been my fault. And if the media were left to their own devices, they could do a lot of damage.

But something about the whole conversation was sitting uneasily with me.

"Why do the Watchers get to decide who should know about magic and who shouldn't?" Because that was effectively what Brian was suggesting, wasn't it? That they act as gatekeepers.

His jaw tightened, and I was pretty sure he'd be able to crack walnuts with his teeth. "Do you want to leave it up to the Order of the Fomori? Somebody needs to manage the fallout from this, and we're best placed to do it."

I winced at the mention of the Order, but I couldn't quite bring myself to agree that the Watchers were the best option. My conversation with Killian from the night before replayed itself in my head, and I once again wondered where the Watchers truly sat on the scale of good to evil.

Before I could say anything further, Brian's phone buzzed on the table. He grabbed it, covering the screen with his hand, but not before I caught sight of a familiar number – Teagan's number.

"Excuse me," he said, standing. "I need to take this."

Questions raced through my mind as Brian strode from the room, waiting until he hit the doorway before raising the phone to his ear.

What was Teagan calling Brian for? If she'd simply been checking that I'd followed through on my promise, surely he'd just have called her back when we were finished or answered the phone here?

Without really thinking, I stood and crept to the

still-open doorway. Trying to appear casual in case Brian was just outside the room, I peered out.

Brian had already made it to the far end of the corridor. I heard him ask, "Are you there yet?" Then he disappeared around a corner.

I frowned, even more suspicious now. Teagan had said she was going on a research project for work, hadn't she? She definitely hadn't said anything to imply that work was for the Watchers.

Chewing on my lip, I debated my options. Sit back down at the table and wait patiently for Brian to return, or...

Brian clearly knew what Teagan was doing today, so it stood to reason that he might just happen to have some details lying about that an innocent passerby might happen to spot. With that in mind, I casually slipped from the meeting room and headed towards the bathroom. The one that I may or may not have seen while waiting outside of Brian's office.

Heart pounding in my chest, I stopped outside the office door and looked around to confirm I was alone. I tried the handle, but it didn't budge.

Dammit. I'd forgotten Brian had locked it after retrieving his stupid folder. What did I do now?

The good angel on my shoulder was having a little freak attack, telling me I needed to go back to the waiting room before somebody caught me. The devil's advocate on my other shoulder was filing her nails and casually pointing out that the Watchers were exploiting Teagan's current vulnerability for their own means. As a good friend, I was duty bound to find clues so I could look out for her well-being.

The debate lasted less than a second. I released the handle and took a slow breath. Closing my eyes, I held my hands over the keyhole.

Killian regularly assigned me homework from our magic lessons. There was still a vast difference in the strength of magic here in our world compared to the dreamscape, but I'd gotten quite good at manipulating small objects with air as I worked on my precision. I put that practice to use now, directing air currents through the door's locking mechanism until I heard a telltale click.

"Now, I might be new around here, but I'm pretty sure that's not your office."

CHAPTER SIX

Guilt was no doubt written all over my face as I turned to find Pete standing behind me. Amusement glinted in his brown eyes as he quirked an eyebrow. I shifted my body in a pathetic attempt to block the name plaque on the door from view.

"Oh, hey, Pete. I was just looking for the bathroom. You don't happen to know where it is, do you?"

He crossed his arms and leaned against the wall, amusement now tugging at the corner of his lips too. "You were looking for the bathroom behind a locked door that just happens to be Brian's office?"

"Oh, is this Brian's office? I..." Trailing off, I gave a resigned sigh. We both knew I wasn't fooling anybody.

"What's going on, Ais?"

Despite his relaxed posture, I didn't miss the crease of concern that furrowed his brow. I knew Pete would never rat me out to the Watchers, but could I trust him?

"I think Teagan is keeping something from me. I wanted to make it up to her for not being as supportive as I should have been about the training, but she's gone off on some research project she never ever mentioned. And now she's having secret conversations with Brian, and I don't trust him or the Watchers. And..." I ran out of steam, my shoulders slumping dejectedly.

Pete waited until he was sure I had it all out of my system before speaking. "It's not like Teagan to spare you any details if she has a new project to share. Normally she'd have burned the ears off you by now."

I nodded, half relieved he didn't dismiss my concerns outright, half worried that it only confirmed my fears.

The frown lines in Pete's brow deepened as he considered this. "I've only spoken to her in passing while I've been here training. And I'm still trying to figure my way around all these new instincts. But my wolf hasn't sensed any immediate danger around her, I don't think, at least."

The uncertainty in his voice made my heart ache, and I was momentarily distracted from my concerns about Teagan. It was clear he was trying hard to understand this new relationship with his wolf. I couldn't imagine how confusing all the new feelings and instincts were to process, but I appreciated him trying reassure me.

Still, the sense that something was amiss stayed with me.

The huge building I was in suddenly felt very small and oppressive. I needed to get out of here and clear my head.

"Can you do me a favour and tell Brian I've left? Tell him I need time to think about what we were discussing."

Pete's eyes scanned my face, though I couldn't have said just what he was thinking. "What are you going to do?"

I attempted a reassuring smile, but if the deepening of his frown was anything to go by, I fell short. "I'm going to think about how to fix things with Teagan before this whole mess drives a permanent wedge between us."

Giving him a feeble wave, I turned and began retracing the path I'd followed with Brian. More than one curious gaze turned my way as I traversed the open-plan office once more. I kept my head down, and thankfully nobody commented on my swift exit.

By the time I made it back to the reception, I had taken two wrong turns that had forced me back on myself, and I was in no mood for the receptionist's resting bitch face glower. I didn't bother with a goodbye before hurrying to the sanctuary of my car.

Even as I increased the distance between me and the Watchers' HQ, the oppressive weight of all the things I still didn't know stayed with me. The thought of going back to an empty apartment just made me feel even worse. So, when my stomach grumbled, I headed for The Wooden Spoon, a small cafe near Teagan's apartment.

At near lunchtime on a Sunday, the cafe was already packed with people enjoying the mouth-watering brunch options – just like I'd planned for me and Teagan. I tried to ignore the pang of jealousy as I ordered a deluxe hot chocolate and found a quiet table at the back of the cafe to drown my sorrows in the mug of sugar.

The place was alive with the buzz of conversation. At the table next to me, two young women giggled and gasped over their antics of the previous night. Listening to them made the ache in my chest grow even stronger. I missed Teagan. I missed days – and nights – like that with her. But most of all, I missed the surety that our friendship was unbreakable.

I was suddenly overwhelmed with the need to fix the growing chasm between us, Watchers be damned. All this tiptoeing around each other had to stop. We'd lay everything out on the table, have a frank conversation, and clear the air once and for all.

With a renewed sense of determination, I dug my phone out of my pocket. But before I could send Teagan a message insisting we talk when she got home, an email notification flashed up on my screen.

Someone calling themselves "Hotboy85" had sent me an email. Funnily enough, it wasn't an address I was familiar with, and my immediate thought was spam. Then the message preview loaded, and to my surprise it was neither a dodgy marriage proposal or an offer to bequeath me with millions from a dying man's will. Despite my better judgement – which was probably questionable at best anyway – I clicked into the email.

Pixel by pixel, a picture revealed itself on the screen. Old tombstones appeared, cracked and jagged and covered in moss. The land between the graves lay barren and leached of life and colour, as if the death within the graves had spread to their surroundings.

Frowning, I scrolled down to find a second picture loading. This time a landscape scene revealed itself. It was the same barren land as the previous photo, only this picture showed the remains of an old church in the background. The Church of the Blessed Heart.

I sucked in a breath. *What the hell?*

A final image appeared on the screen as I scrolled down. In an instant, I was transported back to the first day I visited the old church grounds with Teagan. The day that started it all.

I stood beneath a beautiful cherry blossom tree as Teagan excitedly recounted the story of Betty Anne, a local woman who had been accused of witchcraft. After she'd been drowned in a failed attempt to prove the charge, the church refused to allow her to be buried on consecrated ground. Not long after, the parish priest went mad and burned down the church. Rumours circulated that Betty Anne's coven had cursed him for refusing her burial.

Incidentally, the grave we'd stood beside that day – the one I was now looking at on my phone – was the grave of Betty Anne. Nobody knew how it had come to be on the church grounds, and nobody dared check if her body really resided there.

But unlike when I'd stood there with Teagan that day, surrounded by the wild embrace of nature, there was nothing but death in the picture before me. The tree that had guarded Betty Anne's resting spot appeared to have rotted from the inside out, its branches cracked and crumbling. The land around it was the same barren wasteland that had been visible in the other photos. And the small plaque that marked Betty Anne's grave was shattered into tiny pieces.

My heart clenched painfully.

"She was your ancestor, you know."

I jerked my head up, as surprised by the fact that someone had approached without me noticing as by the familiar voice.

Bres stood over me, blond hair mussed in that windswept way that made it look like he'd just put his surfboard away. His vibrant blue eyes sparkled with mischief as he pulled out the chair across from me and dropped into it.

My mouth opened and closed of its own accord until I belatedly realised I was doing an embarrassing fish impression and snapped it shut. "What are you doing here?" I demanded.

The last time I'd seen Bres, he was warning me to stay away from the sons of Carmen, who as it turned out, were conducting ritual sacrifices on behalf of the Order of the Fomori – his employers. At least, that was the last time I knew for a fact I'd seen him. There was still the question of who had carried my unconscious form to safety after I'd killed Dothar and Dain. The memory of that familiar voice hovered at the edge of my consciousness...

Bres gave me a cheeky grin and slouched in the chair, draping an arm over the back. "Can't I check in with old friends?"

"Is that why you saved me from Dub?" I hedged. "Because we're friends?" It was his voice I'd heard that night; it had to have been. But why would he have saved me?

Without even acknowledging the question, he nodded at my phone resting on the table between us. "I see you got my email."

Taken off guard, I looked from the phone to him. "You're Hotboy85?" I gaped at him in disbelief.

He pouted. "Of course! Who else do you know that is this hot?"

I snorted.

The mischief seemed to dim somewhat from his eyes. "I just thought you might be interested to know what happened to your ancestor's resting place. Though I thought the Watchers might have already told you." He shrugged. "Or your friend might have said something."

My breath caught in my chest. Was he talking about Teagan? Did she know something about this? No. He was trying to distract me because he obviously didn't want to answer my question for some reason.

There was no way Teagan would keep something like this from me.

"When were you last at the Church of the Blessed Heart?" I asked, keeping my expression carefully neutral.

"Why? Do you think *I* did this to send you a message?"

"No. I think you're playing a game, and I want to know what it is. I know it was you who carried me out of the ritual circle that night. What I don't know is why."

He smiled as he straightened in the chair, clearly preparing to leave. "As much as I quite like the image of me as a knight in shining armour, I'm afraid I don't know what you're talking about."

Yes, he did. It was clear from the tightening around his eyes. So why was he denying it?

A newfound curiosity merged with the innate mistrust I felt any time Bres was around. This was the man who had tricked me into releasing magic – going so far as to stage a car accident and nearly killing us both. He worked for an organisation I trusted even less than the Watchers. And regardless of his level of involvement, he'd known the sons of Carmen were killing people and did nothing to stop it. So, what was different about that night?

"What's your game?"

"Well, I am partial to a bit of poker. Strip poker is my preference, if you're offering." He gave me a cheeky wink and stood.

All hints of mischief disappeared as he gave a pointed look at my phone, still resting on the table. "I don't know about you, but that seems pretty personal to me. Might be a good idea to watch your back."

With that, he turned and left.

CHAPTER SEVEN

Teagan hadn't returned by the time I got back to the apartment, and I was kind of glad. Bres's words still rang in my head, and I couldn't face the conversation I needed to have with her while my thoughts were so scrambled.

Could the damage to Betty Anne's grave really have been a personal attack directed at me?

When we visited the grave, Teagan had jokingly suggested that Betty Anne might be related to me. The letters of her surname had faded so that only an O'M were still visible. While it wasn't out of the realm of possibility that she had, in fact, been right, I had little else to go on other than Bres's word. And I already knew how much that counted for.

It was very possible that Bres was lying to encourage me to make connections where none existed. Though what he hoped to achieve from it, I had no idea. If he wasn't lying, I could think of one person in particular who might want to send me a less than friendly message.

With that thought, I hurried to switch on every light in the apartment. Even with the daylight streaming in through the windows, shadows danced ominously around the room. My chest tightened and I swallowed hard against the panic that was trying to claw its way up my throat.

Dub wasn't here. Bres was playing games with me, just like he always did.

I repeated that over and over in my mind like a mantra. Still, my palms were uncomfortably sweaty as I stood in the centre of the empty living room and tried to decide what to do with the rest of my day – other than dissolve into a bumbling mess.

Maybe a run? Yes. It was a nice, fresh day. A run somewhere crowded would be the perfect way to blow off some cobwebs.

Hurrying to my room a little quicker than necessary, I got changed out of my interview clothes. The search for my running trainers stopped me in my tracks as I tried to remember the last time I'd used them.

The bottom of the wardrobe yielded no result, so I stretched up on my tippy-toes to feel blindly along the top shelf. My hand hit something solid and knocked it flying. I ducked as a green object fell straight for my head.

A thud sounded, and I looked down to see a small rectangular bundle at my feet. It was wrapped in green silk fabric, a smudge of dirt the only flaw on the otherwise pristine material. My stomach lurched.

Slowly, I bent down and picked up the bundle. My fingers trembled as I unwrapped the green sash to reveal an old leather-bound book. *The* book. The one Declan Bannon, head of the Order of the Fomori, had given me when he tricked me into releasing magic.

That familiar shame heated my cheeks as I ran my fingers over the place where a title had once been. It was long worn away now, though I knew from memory that the pages of the book were unnaturally pristine given its obvious age.

After realising the truth – that I'd been tricked and hadn't in fact stopped an evil race from returning – I'd been numb, in shock. It wasn't every day you were forced to accept that magic is real and you've just unleashed it on an unsuspecting Ireland. Despite that, I'd had enough sense to gather up the objects I'd used for the ritual, including the book. When I'd returned to the apartment, I'd wrapped it all up and shoved it to the furthest recess of the wardrobe so that I wouldn't have to look at the proof of my stupidity again.

Until now, that was.

I stared at the book, unable to tear my eyes away. The draw I felt to it was unmistakable, though I couldn't quite explain what drove the feeling. The book was written in an ancient form of gaeilge that I couldn't have understood even if I'd paid more attention in school. Still, the tug was strong and insistent.

Without thinking about what I was doing, I flipped

open the cover. Maybe it was a need to face my mistakes head on or just me being a glutton for punishment, but I had to see the ritual again.

The pages were rough beneath my fingers as I carefully turned them. Beautiful flowing penmanship covered almost every inch of the available white space, and I found myself mesmerised by the words even though they might as well have been hieroglyphics for all the sense they made to me. As I neared the page with the ritual, I hesitated. The page I was on was but a turn or two away from my intended destination, but I found myself riveted by the lone paragraph at its centre. Something filled me with an inexplicable desire to hear the words aloud, and clumsily, I attempted to sound them out.

My head snapped back as my whole body suddenly went rigid. Words flowed from my mouth in a voice that was not my own. The pages of the book began flicking past rapidly, and the air around me grew charged.

Try as I might, I could not stop the stream of words from coming. My vision blurred and the world swam.

Then, just as suddenly as it began, it stopped.

My vision cleared in a blink, and the words that were tumbling from my mouth simply dried up as if they'd been little more than my imagination. The pages of the book fluttered on the remnants of a breeze until they lay open once more on the very first page.

My mouth dropped open in shock as I stared at the words, now as legible to me as my own handwriting.

Familiar words jumped off the page: magic, Tuatha Dé Danann, Guardian. I sucked in a breath.

Was I hallucinating? Had my encounter with Bres finally pushed me over the edge to the psychotic break that had surely been threatening for the last few weeks since this whole mess began?

With a kind of numb detachment, I started reading.

"Dearest daughter of my daughters. It is my hope that you will never need these teachings, that what we fear may come to pass shall simply pass us by. We are living in turbulent times, and the balance is being threatened in a way that we can no longer allow to continue.

"The leaders of the Tuatha Dé Danann are all in agreement that drastic measures must be taken to prevent the Fomorians from completing the Claiming and taking control of the magic. The measures required are drastic and require great sacrifice from us all. But I fear – for you more than others. For it has been decreed that should this sacrifice be required, our family line is best placed to act as a Guardian to the magic in the generations to come.

"I wish time allowed for me to speak more fully with you on this so that you might one day understand why this is all necessary. For now, just know that every-thing you might need to fulfil this role, you already carry inside you. This book is the legacy that I, and those others living of our line, have put together to help guide you where we cannot. It includes a failsafe to undo our actions should our decision prove to be the wrong one. I hope with every fibre of my being that both this book and the failsafe are an unnecessary measure.

"But no matter what comes to pass, know we are with you and you are loved. Be safe my child."

A lump settled in my throat as I ran my fingers over the last lines. A cool dampness coated my cheeks, though I hadn't even realised I was crying. My ancestors had written this book for me? They knew they'd likely have to sacrifice their lives and their only priority was to help their future generations.

As I turned the pages with a newfound awe, I could see the subtle shifts in handwriting where different people had provided their thoughts, experiences, and insights. All of it was legible to me now, as if the words I'd been compelled to speak were a spell to translate the text.

A vague memory flirted at the back of my mind. When the book had first come to be in my possession, I remember feeling drawn to a particular page. I couldn't say for sure if it had been the page with the spell, but something in my gut told me it had, that the book had been trying to guide me all along.

Could this all have been avoided if I'd just listened to my instincts? My throat burned at the thought. How much pain could have been avoided? How many deaths prevented?

But if I hadn't released magic, Killian would still be in that god-awful, never-ending stasis. Could I really wish that for him? And now that I was aware of the life and energy that surrounded me, would I really want to go back to my ignorance?

I pushed the thoughts away, focusing my attention back on the book as I flicked once more to the ritual. The regret I expected to feel never came. So, for the first time since this whole mess began, I took a deep breath and let go of all the guilt I'd been carrying.

It was only as I flicked past the ritual that I noticed the rest of the pages in the book were blank. Sorrow filled me as I realised what that meant for the women who had spilled their words onto these pages.

Hugging the book to my chest, I settled down on my bed to read.

CHAPTER EIGHT

Daylight faded as I read. Eventually, the impatient grumbling of my stomach reminded me that I did, in fact, have needs to attend to, and reluctantly I tore myself away from the book long enough to cobble together a cheese sandwich for dinner.

Teagan wasn't home yet, and I still wanted to resolve things between us. So, I settled down to lose myself in stories of mischievous fae, malevolent spirits, and magical power struggles while I waited for her to return.

The stories contained within the book were so fantastical that they read more like fiction than real life. And yet, with each personal account I read, I found parts of my own personality traits mirrored back at me from the pages left by my ancestors. Who were these women who had gone before me? What had their world been like to live in?

My eyes grew heavy with the waning light, and at

some point, between one slow blink and the next, the real world dissolved and the dreamscape appeared.

I frowned, disoriented by the sudden shift. The familiar lush grass cushioned me where I sat, while the sun warmed my skin with its comforting heat. Something felt different this time, however.

It took me a moment to notice the odd weight in my lap, and when I looked down, I found the leather-bound book resting there.

How had it crossed over to the dreamscape with me? I hadn't even thought that was possible.

As I gingerly ran my fingers over the cover, possibilities formed in my mind. Could I bring other things here, or was the book different somehow? Maybe I could test it out and if it worked on mundane things, I could bring something to make Killian's time here more enjoyable.

The thought had only just occurred to me when the man himself appeared in the distance. I watched his relaxed stride as he approached and wondered about his life here. Was he happy?

As he came to a stop in front of me, Killian's eyes landed on the book in my lap. "You didn't have to bring me a present."

Have to? Maybe not. But I found, now that the idea was in my head, I really wanted to.

I held up the book so he could see it better. "It's the book Bannon gave me. The one I used to release magic."

Killian stilled. His expression was unreadable, but I caught a flicker of something in his eyes. Fear?

"You trying to find a way to put the genie back in the bottle?"

I frowned. Was that what he thought? That I'd put him back in stasis?

"No. It hadn't even crossed my mind," I said honestly. "I'm guessing it wouldn't be easily done anyway."

"Not unless you were willing to sacrifice everyone you loved."

This time I didn't miss the shadows that darkened his eyes, and I instantly felt guilty. Sure, I hadn't meant to bring the book here with me, but I had intended to speak to him about it. I hadn't really considered that the reminder of his past would be difficult for him.

"Did you know the book was written by my ancestors?" I asked tentatively.

He shoved his hands into his jeans pockets and turned away from me to look out over the horizon. "Yes. But not what it contained, specifically."

Somewhat unsure, I held the book out to him. "Would you like to look at it?"

He jerked his head around, and I could see the battle raging on his face.

"It's all translated," I offered. "There was a spell inside that changed the pages so I could read them."

Though, now that I thought of it, Killian would have been able to read the original language given he came from that time. My cheeks flushed a little in embarrassment at my stupidity, but he didn't seem to notice as his eyes remained fixed on the book.

After a long moment, Killian closed his eyes and took a shuddery breath. He shook his head.

I dropped the book back onto my lap and considered my next words carefully. The last thing I wanted to do was poke at old wounds, but I had questions I needed answers to and I didn't exactly have anyone else to ask, so...

"What's the Claiming?"

A jolt went through Killian at my question, and a blank mask snapped into place over his features. "Where did you hear of the Claiming?"

I indicated to the book in my lap, clutching it a little tighter as I suddenly found myself feeling very protective of it. Aside from my ancestor's note at the beginning of the book, there had been no further reference to it. But things didn't get a capital letter for no reason, and Killian's reaction just confirmed that it was something important.

"What does the book say about it?"

"Just that it couldn't be allowed to happen."

His shoulders relaxed at my words, as if he'd been expecting me to say something else. He nodded, though I could tell his attention had shifted from me to some inward thought or memory.

"That's all you need to know. The Claiming can never be allowed to happen. Our ancestors were willing to sacrifice themselves to see to that."

I suppressed a growl of frustration. I was already

well aware of the sacrifices that had been made – even his, though he seemed so determined to discount it. But that told me nothing of real use.

Sure, I could use my wonderful powers of deduction to assume that it somehow involved someone claiming and taking control of magic. I could even deduce that the Tuatha Dé Danann had been trying to stop the Fomorians from doing exactly that. But what did it involve? Could anyone do it? Was it something I needed to worry about happening now the magic was back?

"Maybe if I understand a bit more about it, I can be better prepared if it –"

He cut me off abruptly. "Some things are better left alone."

I recoiled, taken aback. Killian was often exasperated with me, and he never shied away from telling me the hard truths, but he was never short with me.

"I'm sorry." He shook his head and sighed. "This is all just bringing up some … memories."

Not sure exactly what to say, I just bit my lip and nodded. Only a heartless person wouldn't understand how this might be hard for him. The last thing I wanted to do was hurt him. It just felt like I was always on the back foot with this magic stuff, and I was tired of everyone else knowing more than me about what was going on.

But could I really afford to press this and risk alienating yet another person in my life?

I decided to accept the apology and shelve the

conversation – for now at least. There were other just as cheery subjects we needed to discuss.

"Someone destroyed my ancestor's grave."

Killian blinked. Confusion chased away any visible remnants of the past that haunted him, and he stared at me as if he was trying to determine if I'd lost my mind.

"Betty Anne O'Meara," I clarified. "She was buried on the grounds of the Church of the Blessed Heart. Her grave has been smashed to pieces, and all the land around it is dead."

He straightened, turning his body to fully face me. "You think someone is targeting you."

It wasn't a question, but I shrugged with a feigned nonchalance anyway as I hugged my knees to my chest. "That's what Bres implied. It could have been kids joking about, but it seems like a big coincidence considering…"

I trailed off, suddenly realising Killian had once more grown still. The tightening of his jaw was subtle, but I caught the tic of the muscle as he clenched his teeth.

"Stay away from that man, Aisling."

This time it was my turn to snap. "What do you think, that I went looking for him?"

Did he really think I was that stupid? I was well aware that Bres couldn't be trusted. The fact he'd most likely saved me from Dub didn't change that.

"No. That's not what I meant." Killian ran a hand through his hair in clear frustration.

My irritation fizzled away as the fight left me. In a quiet voice I asked, "Do you think it could have been Dub?"

Killian was quiet for a moment; then he came to sit next to me on the grass. His shoulder pressed against mine and his warmth seeped into me. For the briefest moment, I allowed myself to pretend I was safe.

"It's very possible," he said. "Plague and death followed Carmen and her sons everywhere they went. You need to be careful, Aisling. Dub didn't know what you were capable last time. He does now."

CHAPTER NINE

My whole body ached as I rubbed the sleep from my eyes and groggily pushed myself up to sitting. It seemed I'd fallen asleep on the sofa while waiting for Teagan, and if her closed bedroom door was anything to go by, she'd returned at some point but hadn't bothered waking me.

I pushed away the sting of hurt that thought carried and trudged to the bathroom for a shower. I'd gotten an email late yesterday evening about a small law firm in urgent need of a temp paralegal. According to the recruitment agent, there was a high possibility of the role becoming permanent. It was the perfect excuse to brush off Brian's job offer, so I needed to make sure I made a good impression.

Becker & Associates was situated just outside the city centre, in a building that barely seemed larger than the main boardroom at Smith & Mercer. The juxtaposition to my previous employment immediately endeared me to the place, and I crossed my fingers that their clientele didn't include psychotic magic users or dodgy organisations that had evolved from ancient civilisations.

A lady in her late fifties greeted me at the door, her brown eyes sparkling as she gave me a warm smile. "Aisling? Thank you so much for coming on short notice. I'm Mona."

I shook her offered hand and returned her smile. A musty smell tickled my nose as I followed her through the reception area and into a small office beyond. It reminded me of the bookish smell from my favourite childhood library, and I instantly liked the place.

Four desks were spaced out around the room, each in varying states of disarray. A young man with wire-rimmed glasses looked up from one of the neater ones and gave me a shy smile.

"That's Kenneth," Mona said, by way of introduction. "Rochelle, our other paralegal, is on holidays at the moment, but you'll meet her later in the week. Jessica's office is at the back here."

She gestured to a plain wooden door at the back of the room. It had none of the fancy gold plaques or frosted glass windows I was used to seeing, and it fit in perfectly with the unpretentious tone of the space. Though nerves flitted around my belly at facing something new, I didn't have the feeling of hyperalertness that I'd had in Smith & Mercer. In a firm like that, there was always someone waiting to stab you in the back and take your job if you so much as breathed wrong.

Mona came to a stop at an empty desk towards the back of the room. It was neatly organised with folders stacked on one side of the computer. A vase occupied the space on the opposite side and was filled with seven lush red roses. She smiled when she noticed they'd caught my attention.

"It seems somebody wanted to wish you luck on your first day. These were delivered first thing this morning."

My mouth went dry, and I swallowed with effort. "For me?"

She nodded. "Lucky girl."

I stared at the soft velvet petals, unable to tear my eyes away. My hands started to tremble, and I clenched them into tight fists at my side. *It's not the same. The rose Dub sent you was so dark it was almost black. These are red.*

Yes, red like blood.

Conscious of Mona's smile faltering as she took in my expression, I forced a smile of my own. "My friend must have sent them to wish me luck on my first day. She's very thoughtful like that."

Yes, that was the most logical explanation – Teagan had somehow found out about the role and sent them as a show of support. Of course, I had no idea how she'd have known... Maybe it was the recruitment agent? That would be a nice personal touch.

"What a lovely friend." Mona clasped her hands together, her beam returning to full wattage.

She set about getting me comfortable at my desk

and showing me through the system. I soon got lost in the familiarity of the work, and though I got a shiver of unease every time I caught sight of the flowers from the corner of my eye, I forced myself to focus on the rhythmic clicking of my keyboard.

Before long, I had found my flow and was making a nice dent in the meeting notes that needed transcribing. I was so absorbed by what I was doing that when the phone rang, I almost leapt out of my seat.

"Good morning, Becker & Associates," I answered, my "phone voice" kicking in on reflex.

Silence.

"Hello?"

There was nothing, no burst of static or background noise.

Frowning, I looked at the phone, then shrugged and hung up. If it was important, they'd call back.

Sure enough, ten minutes later the phone rang again. This time I glanced down at the caller ID, but it simply showed as "unknown." I answered and was met with the same dead silence.

As I strained to listen for any sound, I thought I caught the slightest hint of someone breathing. Not sure if it was my imagination playing tricks on me, I tried a couple more times to get a reply from whoever was on the other end. When they still didn't speak, I hung up.

Kenneth glanced up from the file he'd had his head buried in all morning. "Everything okay?"

Ignoring the little voice in my head that was

adamantly insisting no, everything was not okay, I smiled. "Must have been a wrong number."

But it was harder to concentrate after that, and with each successive phone call, my nerves grew tauter and tauter.

Unknown caller.

Burst of static.

Unknown caller.

Ominous silence.

Unknown caller.

Unknown caller.

Unknown caller.

By the time the shrill tone of the phone shattered the peace of the office for the tenth time, I was vibrating with tension. I didn't even think before yanking it up from the cradle and shouting, "Who the hell is this?"

Mona and Kenneth turned in unison to gape at me, and a burst of static crackled through the phone.

"Hello? Can you hear me? – Sorry, terrible recept –"

The line cut off to abrupt silence that was echoed back at me by the mortifying quiet that filled the office. My cheeks turned to furnaces as I slowly put the phone down.

"Em, I think my blood sugars might be a little low. Would it be okay if I take my lunch now?"

Mona's kindly eyes crinkled with concern, but she simply nodded.

As I grabbed my bag and coat, the roses once more caught my eye. I scowled. How the hell had I let a bunch of goddamned flowers turn me into a basket case? If I wasn't careful, they'd be paying me to leave, not offering me a longer contract. I needed to get my shit together.

Not wanting to be late back to the office, I made my way to a nearby café. I ordered soup and a sandwich and found a table at the back, as far away from other customers as possible. My stomach was still churning from the stress of the morning, but I forced myself to take a few bites of my food before finally giving up and pushing it away.

I debated heading back to the office so I could get working on that good impression I really needed to make. But I had told Mona my blood sugars were low; would it look strange if I came back too quickly? Maybe I'd give it five more minutes.

Since the last thing I needed right now was to spend five minutes alone with my thoughts, I reached into my bag and pulled out my ancestor's book. Reading a book about magic probably wasn't an ideal distraction, all things considered, but I figured a page or two couldn't hurt. Besides, Killian's evasiveness had only made me more determined to learn more about the Claiming.

With a surreptitious glance around to make sure no one was paying too close attention to me or my book, I began flicking. I'd only gone about five pages when I stopped.

The pages were different.

Where originally the first part of the book had

given insight into the most prominent types of mythological creatures in existence during the time of the Tuatha, now it seemed to focus on the Fomorians – their structure, key players, and the threat they posed to Ireland. I read eagerly, excited to maybe find some insight that could help me understand the current day Order of the Fomori better.

I quickly became engrossed in a story about the uneasy truce made between the Tuatha and the Fomorians. A female and male had been chosen from each respectively and wed in an arranged marriage. If anything Bres told me could be trusted, they'd been his ancestors. When my phone rang, I was startled back to reality. I pulled it out to see Pete's name on the screen.

"Hey," I answered. "What's up?"

There was a hesitant pause before he answered, "I'm not too sure. I think something's wrong."

CHAPTER TEN

My breath caught in my throat, and I gripped the phone tighter. "What do you mean something's wrong?"

"I don't know," Pete repeated, frustration clear in his tone. "My wolf is on edge, but everything's clouded. Before, whenever I sensed danger, there'd always be a clear indication of who it involved. Now, I can just sense ... something. Every time I try to focus on it, it all becomes muggy."

Okay. Nothing to panic about, I told myself, forcing my hand to relax its grip.

"Something" didn't mean anyone was in imminent danger. I mean, sure someone had sent flowers to a job nobody knew I was starting. And yes, my ancestor's grave had been damaged. But that could all be coincidence. There was no guarantee it had anything to do with the weird feeling Pete was having – or the magic-wielding homicidal maniac that was possibly out there somewhere plotting revenge against me for his brother's deaths.

A hysterical laugh bubbled up in my throat, and I swallowed it back with effort. *Concentrate, Aisling.*

With a quick glance at the time on my phone, I considered my options. "I need to get back to work, Pete. Can you meet me later for dinner? Maybe if we talk it through together, we can figure out what's bothering you?"

He sighed. "Yeah, I can do that. Sorry, Aisling. I don't mean to be worrying you. I'm sure it's nothing, but my wolf is restless and it's making me antsy."

"You've nothing to be sorry for. This is new to us all, and I don't think it would be wise to ignore your instincts."

We said goodbye, and I gathered up my stuff to head back to the office. I had no idea how I was going to focus for the rest of the workday, but I was going to have to find a way. Otherwise I might have no choice but to start taking Brian's job offer seriously.

I pasted what I hoped was a relaxed expression onto my face as I walked back into the office – sugar levels all topped up, crazy lady back under control. The warm smile Mona gave me eased a little of the tension that had tied itself into a tangled knot at the centre of my chest.

"Did you have a nice lunch?"

"It was lovely, thanks." Though in truth I couldn't even remember what flavour the soup was. "I'm ready to get stuck in. Is there anything particular you need help with?"

"Fantastic, dear. You can help me transfer some of our old client files over to the new system." She bustled about, gathering files and passing them to me as she went. "Oh, I almost forgot. Someone left another present for you while you were out. I was in the back, so I didn't see who it was. My, you are a lucky lady today."

Ice flooded my veins. Another present?

Almost against my will, my eyes turned towards my desk. A small black box sat next to the vase of roses. Black satin ribbon wound around it, but I could see no card or indication of what might be inside.

Memories flashed through my mind of a similar black box resting at Teagan's apartment door. My breath froze in my chest as my ribs suddenly forgot how to expand. I gripped the folders tightly to my chest, but it didn't seem to stop my hands from shaking.

Mona looked at me expectantly, and though I wanted nothing more than to turn and flee, I took the dreaded few steps to the desk.

A numb sense of detachment settled over me as I placed the folders down and reached out a hand to lift the lid from the box. Slowly, and with an almost resigned sense of dread, I revealed the contents.

Dirt.

I blinked in confusion at the parched soil that filled the box. What the –

My attention snagged on something sticking up at the centre. Tentatively, I reached in to pull it out. A piece of stone came free in my hand. For a moment, I just stared at it, brow furrowed. Was this it?

Then a suspicion took form in my mind. I knew before I even turned the stone over what I'd find, and sure enough, there as a roughly carved 'O' on the other side. It was a piece of Betty Anne's grave.

The stone fell from my hand and clattered to the desk. I stumbled backwards as if putting distance between me and it would lessen the threat that was terrifyingly clear.

I can find you.

"Is everything okay, dear?"

I barely heard Mona's question as I grabbed my coat and bag. "I'm so sorry," I mumbled, hurrying to the door. "I have to go."

The drive home was a blur. Only when I pulled into the underground car park for Teagan's apartment block and released the death grip I had on the steering wheel did I realise just how lucky I'd been to get back without causing an accident.

I was a mess. My hands were trembling and sweaty, and it felt like a steel band was being pulled tight around my chest. And that was even before I'd navigated the concrete expanse that lay between me and the stairwell.

Refusing to let myself be cowed, I climbed out of the car and hurried towards the entrance to the apartments. A car door slammed somewhere in the car park.

I bit back a yelp and hurried my steps. By the time I made it up the stairs to the elevator, I was all but hyperventilating. I smashed the button for the third floor.

When the elevator came to a stop, I barely waited for the doors to finish opening before I squeezed out and ran to the apartment. I fumbled awkwardly with my keys, dropping them in my haste to get inside.

As I crouched down to retrieve them, the door swung open. Teagan looked down at me, her face a mask of surprise.

"Aisling? What's going on?"

Oh, nothing too serious, I thought, rising to my feet. *I just seem to have gotten myself a little stalker who may or may not be a murdering psychopath who can move through shadows.*

As the words ran – somewhat hysterically – through my head, a memory came to me of walking into Teagan's apartment to find Dub there waiting for me. Of Teagan coming home, and the fear I'd felt that I was going to get my best friend killed.

Oh god, what the hell had I been thinking coming back here? What if I'd led him here again? What if I'd reminded him how easy it had been to get to me through my friends. Dread washed over me.

"Earth to Aisling." Teagan waved a hand in front of my face to get my attention. She looked perplexed.

I realised she was waiting for an answer from me about something, and I scrambled to form a coherent thought through the panic that had become a cacophony in my head.

"Sorry. I'm not feeling the best. Things didn't go too well at the job." I needed to get out of here. I needed to think.

"The job with the Watchers? I didn't realise you'd started already?"

Distracted from my train of thought, I blinked at her in confusion. "What? Oh no, I'm not working for the Watchers. I had a temp job, but something came up. I had to leave."

She frowned. "Why are you still taking temp jobs? The job Brian is offering is permanent, isn't it?"

"Maybe we don't all want to be lapdogs for the Watchers." The words were out of my mouth before I'd even had a chance to think. There was no bite behind them, but Teagan stepped back as if I'd slapped her.

Without saying anything, she turned and disappeared into the apartment, leaving the door open for me to do with it as I would.

Every part of me yearned to go after her, to fix this chasm growing between us. But how could I? How could I put her in danger again? My eyes burned as frustration threatened to bring me to tears. I shouldn't have come back here. I needed to leave.

With a strangely hollow feeling in my chest, I pulled the door to the apartment closed, fixed my bag on my shoulder, and made my way back to the elevator.

Where could I go that wouldn't possibly put someone I cared about in danger? Pete had his wolf now, and I had no doubt he'd both be able to defend himself and allow me to stay with him. But the memory of him strapped to that standing stone, separated from his wolf and looking close to death, was too fresh in my mind to even consider that avenue. I couldn't go to my mam's and risk exposing her to the insanity my life had become either. I had no one.

The only thing I could think to do was keep moving, so I made my way back down to the car park, feeling more alone than I ever had before.

As I emerged from the stairwell, my pulse quickened. The overhead fluorescent lights cast eerie shadows between the sea of cars that filled the concrete space. There was no sound aside from that of my ragged breathing and clipped steps as I hurried to my car.

My hands were still trembling so badly that when I reached into my pocket for my car keys, I fumbled and dropped them. They clattered to the ground and disappeared under the edge of my car.

I swore and crouched down, stretching my arm under to feel for them. When my fingers closed around the cold metal, I sighed in relief.

The lights flickered, and everything went dark.

"Did you miss me?"

CHAPTER ELEVEN

The scream that welled up inside me lodged in my throat as paralysing fear took hold. I knew that voice. Knew who it belonged to.

Complete and utter blackness surrounded me, and when Dub spoke again, his words seemed to come from everywhere and nowhere at once. "Did you think we'd stay away forever, Guardian? Did you think you were safe?"

Terror tightened my chest until it was nearly impossible to breathe. I clenched my fingers around my keys, using the bite of metal into my skin to focus my thoughts. Oh so slowly, I rose to my feet.

"It took you long enough to show up."

A deep, velvety laugh wrapped around me, and the darkness dissipated until I found myself staring at a broad chest clad in a black t-shirt. I swallowed hard.

The last thing I wanted to do was look my nightmares in the eye, but I forced myself to tilt my head up to take in Dub's face. As before, shadows swirled around his almost delicate bone structure. It was both disorientating and mesmerising. Through those shadows, his piercing black eyes fixed on me, pinning me to the spot even as every instinct in my body demanded I run.

"We needed time to prepare." He reached out as if to touch my cheek, and I flinched away.

Instinctively, I reached out to pull magic to me ... and was met with an empty void.

Dub's life force was a blazing beacon before me, and my own was ever present in my consciousness. But there was nothing else. It was like I was standing in an echo chamber with nothing around me for miles.

The blood in my veins turned cold as I realised the concrete cage of the underground car park was blocking my access to magic. How could I fight him if I couldn't use magic?

Panic choked me.

"Prepare for what?" I asked, scrambling for time so that I could think.

He tilted his head to the side and frowned. "For your punishment, of course. Did you think we wouldn't make you pay?"

We? He'd said that more than once now, hadn't he? But his brothers were dead – the Watchers confirmed it.

Unless they lied...

I risked taking my eyes off Dub for just a split second to look around in case Dothar and Dain were, in fact, waiting to step out of the shadows. But we were alone.

Dub was crazy, I reminded myself. I needed to stop listening to what he was saying and figure a way to get the hell out of this mess.

Once more, I reached out in a desperate search for any magic that might aid me. The layers of concrete that surrounded us acted as effective a buffer as I'd ever encountered, and though I had a vague sense of the energy waiting beyond it, I couldn't draw it to me no matter how hard I willed it.

Which left only my siphoning powers.

My stomach gave a sickening twist at the thought of history repeating itself. Dub was evil, and I'd be lying if I said the world would be a better place with him alive. But being responsible for his death was a whole different thing.

I didn't have to kill him though, did I? Killian had said my power could be used simply to disable an opponent's magic. Could I control it enough to draw the line between that and draining his life force?

"We'll make it special, of course," Dub continued, apparently oblivious to my inner turmoil. "You'll come back with me to the Church of the Blessed Heart, and we'll rewrite that night. We'll make it how it should have been."

I couldn't help it – I barked out a laugh of disbelief. "You're insane. Do you really think I'd go anywhere with you?"

He tilted his head, a look of confusion visible

beneath the swirling shadows. "But you must. She wants to meet you."

My blood ran cold. She?

Any doubts I harboured about using my siphoning powers against him vanished in an instant. There was no way I was going anywhere with him, and I certainly didn't want to meet whoever "she" was.

Fighting to contain my ever-rising terror, I held out a trembling hand to him. "Okay. I'll go with you."

There was an almost innocent trust in his expression as he reached out to take my hand. I'd have felt bad if it wasn't for the fact I knew he was going to kill me.

His touch made me want to recoil in revulsion, but I forced myself to grip his hand. Tapping into that place at the very centre of my core, I reached out for the energy that burned like an ice-cold fire within him, and called it to me.

The rush was instantaneous. Dub's energy was more potent than even his brothers' had been – though I'd been at the brink of death the last time I'd unknowingly embraced my siphoning ability. The heady effect sent the world spinning and my body felt lighter, as if I was suddenly floating off the ground.

A sharp crack across my cheek shattered my hold on the magic and sent me stumbling backwards. Tears filled my eyes and blurred my vision as pain radiated through my skull.

"Did you think I wouldn't remember your little tricks, Guardian?" Dub sneered as he loomed over me, looking more terrifying than ever before. "Did you think we wouldn't be ready for them this time? Just like we were with your wolf."

I blinked rapidly, trying to clear my vision and took another step back, away from the cold fury that emanated from him. In truth, no. It hadn't occurred to me that he'd be prepared for my siphoning ability; I'd been too wrapped up in trying to accept this horrific part of myself. And what did he mean about Pete?

Dub backhanded me across the cheek again, and this time the force was enough to send me to the ground. Stars exploded behind my eyes and I let out an involuntary sob. Despite the futility of it all, I clambered to my hands and knees and tried to crawl towards my car. If I could just get to it, maybe I'd stand a chance.

But I didn't make it that far.

Shadows twined in my hair and yanked my head back. Almost lovingly, they slid around my neck and caressed my cheek, sending a wave of revulsion roiling through me.

"You tricked me. You let me believe we could have had something special," Dub whispered, his breath brushing the back of my neck. "But all the time you were one of *them*."

Tears burned my eyes as I scrabbled for purchase on the cold concrete. My fingers knocked against something hard, and my breath stalled. My keys. When had I dropped them?

The shadows allowed me little or no leeway as they

pulled my hair taut and set my scalp on fire. I fought to breathe through the pain, and slowly, so as not to attract Dub's attention, I pulled the keys to me so that they protruded from between my fingers.

Then I struck.

Clumps of my hair wrenched out from the root as I twisted my body and slashed out. Pain blazed through me, but it was worth it when my makeshift weapon hit home. The keys gouged a jagged line down the side of Dub's face. Blood poured from the wound, and his left eye was such a mess I didn't know if he could see from it. I didn't wait to find out.

With the surprise of my attack, Dub's shadows retreated to protect him. As soon as they loosed their grip on me, I turned and ran for the car park exit. I took what little energy I'd managed to siphon from Dub and directed it into my muscles, sending a burst of energy into my cells.

As I ran, I hit the button on my keys that would raise the barrier. Slowly, the security shutters began to rise and daylight seeped in through the growing gap – a beacon of safety that called to me. I lunged for it.

Shadows locked around my neck and jerked me to a stop. The force nearly crushed my windpipe, and I let out a strangled gasp as they tightened, reducing the natural flow of oxygen to a mere trickle.

I clawed at the shadows, desperately trying to loosen their hold. But there was nothing for my fingers to gain purchase on. The shadows were at once insubstantial and yet so terrifyingly real.

Footsteps sounded behind me as Dub approached. This time, it was his fingers that wrapped in my hair and yanked my head back. Another shadow snaked around and covered my mouth – not that I had air enough to scream anyway.

"I think it's time that you and I get moving. There's much to do before sunset."

My vision swam as more shadows danced around me. The ground disappeared from beneath my feet and I was suddenly weightless, being moved towards the daylight I'd so desperately wanted to reach. Darkness crept in around the edges of my vision as the lack of oxygen made it hard to focus. I blinked sluggishly.

As we crossed through the security gate, I felt the last strands of consciousness slip from my grasp. *At least Teagan will be safe now,* I thought.

Then I felt it.

The magic.

It returned in a rush as we emerged from beneath the concrete structure of the car park, the vibrant buzz of energy that at some point over the past few weeks, I'd grown used to feeling.

With one last pathetic effort, I called it to me. It flooded me and rejuvenated my aching body, but it wasn't enough to fully counter the ongoing oxygen deprivation. I had just enough coherent thought left to direct the energy towards my muscles and give a pitiful yank against Dub's shadowy hold.

To my shock, I tumbled to the ground, landing with a jarring thud that made even the darkness of my vision swim. The roar of a car engine filled my ears, and then the screech of breaks followed by a bone-crunching thud.

I blinked in confusion, willing the darkness to recede from my consciousness. Had that car always been beside me?

God, I was so tired. My eyes fluttered closed again as the last of magical energy left me. Somewhere close by a car door opened, and then I was being jostled about.

"Dammit, Aisling, wake up."

Blearily, I cracked my eyes open to see Bres's handsome features pinched tight with concern. And then oblivion took me.

CHAPTER TWELVE

The first thing that told me I was still alive was the pain; the second was Bres's face hovering above me as I opened my eyes. Angelic-looking he might be with that cute face and those dazzling blue eyes, but I knew better, and I was pretty sure he wasn't making it to heaven. Then again, maybe I wasn't either.

I bolted upright and immediately regretted it as my skull split in two and the world swam. Bres placed a hand on my shoulder and gently but firmly pressed me to lie back down. I tried to resist, but it was like the messages weren't sending from my brain to my muscles.

"Where am I?" I demanded in a hoarse croak.

The soft surface beneath me wasn't the hard concrete of the car park I remembered lying on, but rather a plush beige sofa. I peered over Bres's shoulder and caught a glimpse of a familiar skyline through a panoramic window. We were in the city somewhere. But where, and how had I gotten here?

"You're at my place," Bres answered. "I know you're desperate to get into my bed, but passing out on me my while I'm rescuing you is so cliché."

I gaped at him, and he grinned unrepentant.

A mental head-to-toe scan told me I was still wearing the same clothes beneath the soft white throw that covered me. My top had gone stiff in places where blood had streamed onto it – presumably from my lip that was split and throbbing – and dried in. It was minor in comparison to the unending ache that appeared to be my body, but it made me shudder in revulsion.

"What happened?" Aside from me almost being killed – again.

Bres stood from his crouched position and settled into an armchair across from me. "I knew it was only a matter of time before Dub made his move. Unfortunately, that apartment complex of yours has a pretty decent security system, so I had to twiddle my thumbs outside until he decided it was time for a little field trip. Then I introduced him to my car."

"You ran him over?" I couldn't keep the incredulity from my voice, but I winced as the effort of speaking caused my throat to burn.

Bres's grin widened. "My foot may have slipped on the accelerator." He sat forward and rested his elbows on his knees, growing serious. "He's not dead. Which means he won't stop coming for you."

I pushed myself up to sitting. My body protested at the movement, but I felt far too vulnerable lying there. And as Bres's words hung in the air between us, the last thing I needed was to feel more vulnerable than I already was.

"He's not the only one, is he?" I spoke almost to myself, remembering Dub's words about the woman who wanted to meet me.

Bres nodded, assessing me. "What do you know about Carmen?"

I swallowed and then winced at the sharp pain it triggered. "Mother of the year who raised three homicidal sons. Tried to take over Ireland and killed herself in a huff when things didn't go her way?"

He let out a humourless chuckle. "You've been well informed."

Killian had filled me in on the story of Carmen and her sons when we'd finally figured out who was sacrificing the Watchers of Danu. Of course, I wasn't stupid enough to reveal my source to Bres.

"Dub and his brothers were planning on bringing Mommy Dearest back from the dead," I said, pointedly ignoring the curious glint in his eyes. "It seems *somebody* encouraged them to commit some ritual sacrifices to gather the power to do it."

Bres simply raised an eyebrow, unfazed by my not-so-subtle accusation. "It seems *somebody* might have assisted with the last two deaths they needed."

My blood ran cold as his words hit home.

That night, Dothur had told me they needed two more sacrifices to bring the total to the required seven. Me and Pete were to have the honours. He had gotten as far as creating the blood circle before all hell broke loose. I didn't know if the full ritual was required in order to gather the power, but I couldn't deny that what Bres said was right – two people had died that night as planned. Because I'd killed them.

This time when I tried to swallow, my mouth was too dry and the lump that had lodged itself in my throat was too large. "Could I get some water, please?"

Bres rose and disappeared into what I could only assume was the kitchen somewhere behind me. With him gone, I took a moment to properly assess my surroundings.

Based on the height we appeared to be at and the luxurious open-plan living area that had been simply but tastefully decorated, I guessed we were in a penthouse apartment somewhere in Dublin city centre. There was little of personal significance that I could see lying around except for a couple of well-worn books resting on a side table, their titles turned away from me.

My eyes fell on the door, and I debated whether or not I should leave while he was gone. I wasn't exactly getting kidnapped vibes from this whole setup, but with Bres I could never really be sure of his intentions. Before I could decide, however, he was back with my glass of water.

"Why did you save me?"

Sheesh, that sounded ungrateful even to me. I cringed.

"I told you I didn't want you dead." He handed me the glass and settled back into the armchair, looking as relaxed as ever.

"You told me the Order needed me alive. You never told me why."

"The Order have their reasons, and I have mine. Sometimes those goals align."

I bit back a growl at the cryptic response and tried a different tack. "Was it you that carried me past the illusion spell that night at the Church of the Blessed Heart?"

He held my gaze for a long moment before looking away. "Yes."

"Why?" I demanded.

For the longest time, I didn't think he was going to answer. Then he gave a resigned sigh. "You're not going to let this go, are you?"

My silence said everything it needed to.

"Fine." He ran a hand through his tousled blond hair and stood. "Let me get us some food from the restaurant next door, and I'll tell you everything after we've eaten."

I watched him leave with thoughts that were more conflicted than ever before. Deep down I'd known that it had been his voice I heard that night, his blue eyes I'd seen. But to have it confirmed...

Bres couldn't be trusted. Saving my life – twice –

didn't change that. My life wouldn't be in danger at all if it wasn't for the fact he'd tricked me into releasing magic. So, why was it getting harder and harder to hate him for that?

Something buzzed suddenly nearby, and I yelped. My heart thundered in my chest as I looked around for the next impending threat, fully expecting Dub to step out of the shadows. It eased only marginally when I spotted my bag on the floor next to the sofa and realised the buzzing was coming from there.

Feeling somewhat silly for being so jumpy, I bent over and picked it up. A hiss of pain escaped my lips as the movement reminded me that my body was still more than a little sensitive, but it didn't stop the rush of relief when the weight of the bag reminded me that I'd been carrying my ancestor's book. Thank god I hadn't lost it.

The insistent buzzing came again, and I hurried to pull out my phone. Teagan's name flashed up on the screen, and my stomach lurched. Was she okay? Had Dub gone back for her?

"Teagan?"

"Aisling, I'm sorry. I really don't want to fight. Can you please come home so we can talk?"

I sagged in relief at the obvious lack of panic in her voice, even as my heart clenched painfully. More than anything, I wanted to accept the olive branch she was holding out to me. But I couldn't.

Dub could still be waiting at the apartment, recovered from whatever damage Bres had managed to inflict on him. And even if he wasn't, anywhere I went, there'd be a risk to the people around me. I'd put Teagan into danger more times already than I could count. I couldn't do it again.

It took more than one attempt for me to form my next sentence, and when I did, something inside me broke. "I'm not coming back to the apartment. I don't want to talk right now. Please don't contact me again." The lump in the back of my throat almost choked me. My eyes burned. "I'll be in touch when I'm ready."

I hung up before she could answer, unable to hold my tears in any longer.

Every part of my being screamed to call her back and say I was joking, that of course I wanted to come home and talk things out. But with the memory of Dub's mangled face and terrifying shadows still fresh in my mind, I knew I couldn't. I sucked in a breath and swiped my hand across my face to dash away the tears. If keeping Teagan safe meant me feeling like crap, then so be it; it was the least I could do for her.

And she wasn't the only one I needed to worry about keeping safe. Dub's words about being ready for the wolf rang in my head. I had no idea what he'd meant, but I couldn't help thinking it had something to do with Pete's earlier call.

Before I could second-guess myself, I typed a quick text to Pete apologising for the short notice but I'd have to cancel our dinner plans. My phone started ringing almost immediately, but I cancelled Pete's call and switched off the phone so that neither he nor Teagan could track me.

With those bridges well and truly up in flames, I put the phone back in my bag and pushed to my feet. I needed to get out of here before Bres returned. Though I was damned if I knew where to go.

CHAPTER THIRTEEN

I walked the streets of Dublin for hours. Though I'd spent much of my life exploring these streets, I'd never felt more lost. Every shadowy alley was a potential hiding place where Dub could be lurking. Every hour that passed was a reminder that I had nowhere to go.

By the time night fell, my nerves were frayed and I was exhausted and aching. The streets had grown progressively quieter as commuters made their way home, and whatever protection their presence had afforded me dwindled. I badly needed a shower, and I wanted to talk to Killian. So, praying that I hadn't left an easy trail to follow, I found a random hotel and checked in for the night.

As I stood under a scalding shower and watched the water sluice over my bruised and mottled skin, it truly hit me how close I'd come to losing my life today.

After all my recent near misses I should have been

a pro at brushing things like this off, but it was suddenly difficult to draw breath as tears burned a track down my cheeks. I sank to the floor and let the water pound down on me until it turned cold. Only then did I take a deep, shuddery breath and rise to my feet. I couldn't hide in this shower forever.

Too tired to bother drying my hair, I sank into the bed that occupied most of the room. I couldn't bring myself to switch off the lights, but exhaustion took me nonetheless.

The moment of darkness before the meadow materialised around me was one of the most terrifying of my life. I was almost hyperventilating when the warmth of the dreamscape touched my skin, and Killian was at my side in an instant.

"Aisling?" He crouched down in front of me, worry darkening his eyes as he tilted my chin up to look at him. "What happened? Tell me what's wrong."

I couldn't stop the tears from coming as relief filled me at seeing him. We might have been in a dream world with my physical body lying defenceless in some random hotel, but for the first time all day, I finally felt safe.

"Hey, it's okay. I'm here." He brushed the tears gently from my cheeks, searching my face, no doubt wondering what the hell had gotten into me.

I took a shaky breath and tried to compose myself, suddenly embarrassed. "He came for me," I managed eventually.

Killian went deathly still, his expression darkening in a way that sent shivers through me. "Dub?"

I nodded. "Get this. Apparently, when I killed Dothur and Dain, I gave him the final two sacrifices he needed to resurrect dear old mammy. He wanted to introduce us."

"Carmen's alive?"

"So he'd have me believe, anyway. I declined his invitation to meet the family."

A muscle twitched in Killian's jaw and he sat back on his heels. Every inch of his body seemed coiled, itching to react to the threat it perceived.

"Tell me exactly what happened."

I started at the beginning, told him all about going to the new job only to find an ominous token waiting for me. Something flickered across his face when I mentioned Pete's lack of clarity around a potential threat, but he didn't interrupt. And when I got to the part about encountering Dub in the car park, his expression shuttered completely, as if not wanting me to see the fury that darkened his eyes to raging storms.

"If it wasn't for Bres, I'd probably be dead," I finished, exhaustion settling over me like a heavy weight.

"What do you mean?"

"Bres was there. He hit Dub with his car and got me away. He admitted to being the one who moved me out of the illusion circle at the Church of the Blessed Heart too. I didn't stick around to let him explain why, but maybe I should have." The last bit I said more to myself as I chewed on my lip. Leaving the apartment had seemed like the right choice at the time. Now, I realised it just left me with a lot of unanswered questions.

"And how exactly was it he knew to be there right when you were attacked?"

I blinked, surprised at the iciness in Killian's tone. "He didn't say it in so many words, but I think he's been following me."

If Killian's expression was anything to go by, that probably wasn't the best way to put his mind at ease.

"I don't like that he's involved in this. If he saved you, it was because it suited his purpose. No other reason."

I bristled. "Do you think I don't know that?

He ran a hand through his hair, yanking it at the roots. My irritation dissipated as he stood and started pacing like a wild animal caught behind the bars of a tiny cage. The frustration that oozed from him was almost palpable.

"I can't protect you out there."

Something inside me warmed at the words, but it cooled just as quickly. Because he was right; he couldn't.

"It's not your job to protect me," I said quietly. It was my own. And wasn't that thought damn terrifying.

Killian slowed his steps and seemed to regain control of the rare show of emotions he'd been displaying. He turned to me, all business once more. "Did you tell Bres where you were going when you left?"

I bit back the smart retort that instinctively came to

mind. "No. He went to get us food and I snuck out. I didn't even know where I was going, so I couldn't have told him if I wanted to."

"Promise me you'll stay away from him."

I hesitated. Though I understood where Killian was coming from, some part of me knew I needed more answers from Bres. If I'd stayed, he might have given them to me, but I was too vulnerable in that moment to consider it an option. Could I honestly say that I wouldn't go back on my own terms, though?

No. I couldn't say that. And I wasn't going to lie to Killian either.

"I'm sorry, I can't do that. I know you're just trying to look out for me, but you need to trust me to make my own decisions."

He let a lot growl of frustration. "It's not your decisions I'm worried about, Aisling. He's a liar and he'll use you to get what he wants, just like he has before. He might have saved you this time, but what about when your usefulness wears out?"

I sighed wearily. "I don't know. But it's not like I have many avenues to turn to, do I? You're stuck here, and the only way I can see you to even ask your advice is to leave my body lying asleep somewhere, vulnerable and unprotected. I can't go to my friends because every time I do. it just increases the chances that I'll get them killed. And based on everything I've seen to date, I'm not convinced the Watchers are any better than the Order. So, tell me, Killian, what should I do? Should I just find a corner somewhere to hide and wait until my own personal bogeyman tracks me down and actually succeeds in killing me? Because you can be damned sure I'm not just going to lie down and play dead."

He opened his mouth to answer but I shook my head, cutting him off before he could speak. "No. If there's any chance that Bres has answers for me, I'm going to get them. You don't have to like it, but you do have to respect my decision."

The muscle ticked at the side of his jaw again, but he gave a sharp nod of his head and came to sit next to me, his body rigid with the tension he appeared to be holding in check.

I took in his profile for a long moment, wondering exactly what he was thinking. Then I gave up wondering and rested my head on his shoulder instead. His warmth seeped into me, and after a few breaths, I felt his body relax. We stayed like that in silence until the dreamscape faded.

CHAPTER FOURTEEN

I rapped on the door to the penthouse apartment and waited. Sounds of movement came from inside and a moment later, the door opened to reveal a shirtless Bres. He wore a pair of faded denim jeans slung low on his hips, and his blond hair was mussed as if he'd only just rolled out of bed.

For one mouth-watering moment, I stared at the hard lines of his muscled shoulders and chest, following them as they tapered into a nicely defined V at the junction with his jeans. I allowed myself that time to appreciate the view, then looked up to meet the cocky grin I knew would be waiting for me.

"Feel free to keep looking," he said with a wink. "That much is free."

I ignored the comment and pushed past him into the apartment. "We need to talk."

Trying to appear confident and sure of myself – when I was anything but – I made my way to the sofa where I'd awoken the previous day and sat. Only when he closed the door did I allow myself to relax into the seat.

"If I recall correctly," he said, dropping into the armchair across from me, "I was more than happy to talk. You were the one who left."

I inclined my head. "I wasn't exactly in the best headspace to talk yesterday, given the circumstances. But I'm here now, and I'm giving you one chance to be honest with me."

He quirked an eyebrow in amusement. "About?"

"You've saved me twice now. Why?"

A heavy silence hung in the room between us, and as the seconds passed, I wondered if he was using the time to think up his next intricate lie or if I'd actually get some honest words from him. Would I even know the difference?

"I've been working towards something for a very long time," he said finally. "And I need you alive for it to work. Your death would be ... inconvenient."

I choked out a humourless laugh. "Gee, thanks. What are you working towards – specifically?"

"I want to make it so the Order can never Claim magic."

My next question froze on the tip of my tongue, and I stared at him. "You what?"

He met my obvious disbelief head on. The sparkle of mischief was gone from his eyes, and he was as serious as I'd ever seen him.

"The Order of the Fomori intend to complete the

Claiming ritual and take full control of the land's magic. Just like their ancestors tried to do before the Tuatha stopped them."

"The Claiming," I whispered, dread settling like a solid lump in my gut.

Bres gave me a knowing look. "You figured out how to translate the book, I take it. Yeah, it was one of the reasons Bannon gave you the book – it contains the ritual. He needed you to release the magic, but he also needs you to unlock the ritual. It will only reveal itself to the Guardian."

I shook my head, whether in confusion or denial I wasn't quite sure. Had Killian known the book contained the ritual? Was that why he'd acted strangely when I asked about the Claiming? Why hadn't he told me?

I pushed the thought aside to examine later. One thing at a time.

"That's why the Order are so concerned about keeping me alive. That's why you've been keeping me safe."

"Yes and no."

Now I really was confused. "I don't understand."

"In this particular case, it suits my goal to comply with the Order's wishes. They need you alive, but so do I if I'm to stop them."

"So, let me get this straight. You say you don't want the Order to Claim the magic, yet you were the one who tricked me into releasing it when it was already safely hidden away. How does that make sense?"

"Yes, because so long as the magic remains unClaimed, there is a possibility that they'll someday succeed. The only way to ensure that never happens is if somebody else Claims it first."

Realisation dawned on me, and I had to dig my nails into my thigh to stop myself from bolting for the door. Killian had been right; it was a mistake to come here. If Bres needed me to uncover the ritual for him, there was no way he'd let me walk out of here a second time.

Clearly reading my panic-stricken expression, Bres chuckled. "Oh, you think I want to Claim the magic for myself? Hell no. I don't want anything to do with it."

Thrown, I searched his face for any sign of deception. It wasn't out of the realm of possibility that this was a power grab on his side. Yet, something rang true in his words.

"If not you, then who else? Please don't tell me you're working for the Watchers now?"

Apparently, that was even funnier than my first suggestion because he laughed even harder. I glared at him. At least one of us was finding this funny.

Finally, he composed himself, wiping an actual tear from his eye. He grew serious and fixed me with a look so intense I squirmed in my seat.

"I want you to Claim the magic."

I blinked stupidly at him as my brain tried to make sense of his words. Maybe Dub's attack yesterday had done more damage than I realised. Had I hit my head at some point?

When I didn't say anything, Bres leaned forward and rested his elbows on his knees. "The ritual that created the Guardian line was a derivative of the Claiming ritual. You might not have full control of the power, but you're the closest link to it that exists in our world today. I'm simply suggesting you take that final step."

"You're insane," I sputtered, shaking my head. "Why the hell would I want to own the magic that I never asked for in the first place?"

"To keep it safe from people like the Order ... and the Watchers." His piercing gaze met mine, no joking or playfulness hiding the sincerity behind his words. "The very fact that you don't want it makes you the perfect person to Claim it. You won't try to use it for your own gain or to hurt others."

I opened my mouth only to shut it again. He was right that no part of me was excited by the thought of getting my hands on that much power. If anything, it sounded like a terrifying amount of responsibility. And the thought of either group getting their hands on it...

"Let me get this straight. The Order want me alive because they intend to somehow make me uncover an ancient ritual for them so they can then swoop in and take all the magic for themselves?"

He shrugged. "That about sums it up."

"So, what if I just refuse to find the ritual?"

"They'll start hurting people you care about until you give them what they want."

I stiffened, anger clenching my jaw tight. "Is that a threat?"

"No. It's an answer to your question. I've worked with these people a long time. I know how Bannon's mind works."

His words snapped me back to the harsh reality behind this conversation. Bres did work with the Order. Which meant he'd been just as involved in all the horrible things they'd done.

"And what makes you any better than them?"

Something I couldn't quite name passed behind his eyes, and he looked away from me. "I'm not. I've done plenty of things that guarantee me a nice toasty finale at the end of this life, but if it means stopping the Order, it'll have been worth it."

"The end justifies the means?"

"Sometimes."

I shook my head. "Not if it means innocent people get hurt."

"And what about the innocent people who will get hurt if the Order succeed?"

Once more I fell quiet. I didn't have an answer to that, and Bres knew it. He sighed and ran a hand through his hair.

"You think I'm a monster, and you're right. My actions over the past decade have more than proven that. I don't expect you to trust me, but I have kept you alive despite your insistence on throwing yourself at death's feet. Bannon will make his move soon, and one way or the other, I will stop him. I'd rather do that with us working together."

Before I had a chance to process the conflicting emotions his words stirred, my phone started ringing in my bag. I blinked in confusion for a moment until I remembered that I'd turned it back on before coming here this morning.

Hurrying to catch it before it stopped ringing, I pulled the phone out of my bag to see Pete's name on the screen. I hesitated, tempted to ignore the call. Then I remembered where I was sitting and that I had no guarantee Bres would let me walk out of here if I refused to help him.

With one wary eye on Bres, I answered. "Hey."

"Aisling, where are you? I've been trying to reach you all night. Teagan is worried sick."

"I'm fine. I just needed some space."

"Look, I spoke to Teagan. It's not safe for you to be alone right now. That research project she went on? The Watchers sent her to a site in Wexford. They wanted her to use her powers to see if she could sense any sign of death. Apparently, it was Carmen's burial place, but the whole area has been destroyed by some kind of weird plague."

I didn't think it was possible for my stomach to feel sicker than it already did, but apparently I was wrong. Teagan had known she was being sent to Carmen's grave and she kept it from me? Sure, I could under-stand not wanting to worry me, but to not even say anything afterwards?

My mind flicked back to the strange news reports I'd found that same day, and I recalled Wexford being mentioned as the first reported site of the disease outbreak. Bres had been right. The trail had been leading my way all along. He'd tried to warn me while my best friend had stayed quiet.

"I have to go," I said, numbly. "You and Teagan need to leave this alone. And stay away from the Watchers."

Blocking out the growl of protest that came through the phone, I hung up. "Carmen's definitely back, then."

Bres quirked an eyebrow. "You knew that already."

I swallowed. "It seems a lot more real to have somebody else confirm it too."

"So, what are you going to do about it?"

My brow scrunched in confusion as I met his challenging gaze. "What do you mean?"

"Dub and Carmen. What are you going to do about them? Are you going to keep running scared until they hunt you down – or are you going to fight?"

CHAPTER FIFTEEN

"You expect me to just walk into the Order of the Fomori headquarters with you?" I gaped at Bres in utter disbelief, and he held my stare unwavering.

"Yes."

"You've just told me that these people want to use me to complete the Claiming, and will do so by force if necessary."

"Yes."

I shook my head in complete and utter bewilderment. "And you think I'd go along with this why?"

"Because none of this will matter if you get yourself killed. It was pure luck that I was there to stop Dub." He held up a hand to halt my protest. "You did an admirable job at fighting back. And if it hadn't been for the underground car park blocking your magic, maybe you would've stood a better chance. But Dub – and Carmen – know your tricks now. He's not going to give you an opportunity to get the upper hand. I can help with that."

I narrowed my eyes and considered him. So far, I'd seen no indication that Bres had any magic. All of my interactions with him had been purely mundane – if irritating as hell. So, how exactly was he going to help – run them over with his car again?

As if he read the thought on my expression, he gave me a wry grin. "Well, I can't help with that exactly. But I know what can. And I can help you get it."

When I simply crossed my arms and waited, he acquiesced. "Over the years, the Order has gathered many objects of power, items they believe may help them achieve their aim. Among these is an ancient artefact of the Tuatha Dé Danann called Dagda's Cauldron. It is a powerful siphoning tool that allows the user to drain magic from another – but without the need for touch."

I thought back to my one and only foray into the Orders' headquarters. In true cliché style, Bannon had revealed a secret room hidden behind a bookcase in his office. Though I'd done much to avoid thinking about that time, I did vaguely remember seeing a small, innocuous-looking cauldron in one of the glass cases. It had been accompanied by a sword and a spear if I remembered correctly.

"How is that different to what I can do?" Not that I had the monopoly on robbing people of their powers, but as he'd already pointed out, Dub now expected it of me.

"The cauldron will allow you to do it without touch. And I think, if you can direct it with your powers, you may actually be able to do it without being in the same room."

Okay, now that sounded appealing. I was pretty sure I never wanted to see Dub again. But could I drain somebody again – kill again? The thought caused bile to rise up in my throat, and I knew the answer was no. Not even somebody as terrifyingly evil as Dub.

"The cauldron's siphoning is different than yours," Bres said softly, watching me with unnerving intensity. "It siphons and stores the magic, but because it doesn't consume it, the person doesn't die. I can't be sure about Carmen, since she's only alive again because of magic, but it won't kill anyone else, merely incapacitate them."

I clenched my fists, fighting the urge to wipe my sweaty palms on my trousers. Bres was already far too aware of my weaknesses; I didn't want him to see how much this particular thought affected me. Instead, I took a moment to calm my skittish heart and think through what he was suggesting.

All we had to do was break into Bannon's secret room, steal an ancient artefact, and use it against two powerful magic users who were intent on seeing me dead. Simple.

Not!

"Why should I trust you?" Because that was the only way I was getting in and out of there – if I trusted him not to screw me over.

Silently, he stood and disappeared into a room on

the far side of the living area. He was back a moment later with a bulging folder in hand. He handed it to me without a word.

I looked from him to the folder, half expecting it to grow teeth and bite me. When nothing happened, I took it from him and flicked it open. Inside sat a haphazard mess of pages. Every sheet seemed to be covered in the same handwriting, the ink on some faded with age, while others were as fresh as if they were written yesterday – which if the date on the top was any indication, they had been.

"What's this?" I looked up at Bres, not comfortable enough to keep my eyes off him for long even if I itched to read the contents.

"All of my notes on the Order of the Fomori. What they've done. What I've done in their name. What they're trying to do now." He sat back down across from me, but though he relaxed into the seat, there was a subtle tension to the way he held himself. "It's your insurance policy. You keep it until we get the cauldron."

"And then?"

His lip quirked up at the corner. "And then, you give it back to me and give me a big sloppy kiss as an apology for doubting my intentions."

I scowled. "What if I don't give it back?"

We stared at each other for a long, intense minute.

"I'm trusting you to," Bres said finally. He shrugged. "I deserve whatever repercussions come from the information in that file, but I need to see this to the end first."

Something about the tightening around his eyes and the way the usual teasing disappeared from his voice made me bite my tongue. I had the oddest feeling that he was being honest with me, and I wasn't quite sure what to do with that.

I looked from him to the file and considered my options. Without knowing what was written in the pages I held, I couldn't be sure they were anything more than grocery lists. An insurance policy isn't worth much if the company insuring you is run by conmen out to screw you for every penny you have. And who would I give it to anyway? The Watchers? The Order? The police?

No, I couldn't rely on Bres's say-so for something this big – even if instinct told me that what was written within these pages was important. I needed more than that to risk stepping into the lion's den.

"I need time to think about it," I said, mentally running through my options.

Bres nodded. "Understandable. Of course, Dub is still out there. And Carmen. If you're too scared to take a stand against them, it's only a matter of time before they come for you. I'll do my best to keep you safe, of course, but you do have an impressive talent for attracting trouble."

I glared at him, bristling at the implied jab. Of course I was afraid of facing Dub and Carmen. What sane person wouldn't be? But that didn't mean I was going to sit around with a giant flashing "victim" sign above my head. And he could get stuffed with his knight in shining armour act too!

"I didn't say I wasn't going to do it," I ground out. "But you can't seriously expect me to trust you just because you've handed me a folder of your Dear Diary scribblings?"

Something that looked suspiciously like amusement chased the shadows from his eyes as he stood. "No. I fully expect you to have a backup plan that will result in me being strung up by my balls if I screw you over in any way. Now, why don't you get working on that while I make us some breakfast?"

And with the gauntlet laid down, he disappeared into the kitchen and started clattering about with pots and pans. It seemed he wasn't making the mistake of popping out this time, lest I pull another disappearing act. He was right though; I needed to use whatever time I had to myself to plan.

Questioning all of my life choices up to this point, I pulled out my mobile and fired off a text before I could rethink my decision:

If you don't hear from me in an hour, send the Watchers to this address:

Number 7 King's Street

With a glance towards the kitchen to make sure Bres was still occupied, I turned my attention to the folder in my lap. I might not have time to read it all, but I could do something even better – something that would allow me to read it later. By the time he walked back into the room carrying two plates loaded with food, I'd taken photos of more than half the pages. I switched off my phone and slipped it back into my bag before he could notice what I was up to.

Bres nudged a small side table my way with his foot, then placed one of the plates in front of me. Succulent sausages, eggs, and hash browns. My mouth watered.

"Dig in." He gave me one of his cheeky winks. "You're going to need your strength."

CHAPTER SIXTEEN

As I stood facing the headquarters of the Order with Bres at my side, I couldn't help but feel like I had a giant "idiot" sign flashing over my head. Last time I'd been here, Bres had gone "missing" and I'd come to the Order for help to rescue him. I'd walked out with the promise of that help, but only after I'd agreed to conduct one little ritual for Bannon, the head of the Order.

For the record, it's never just a "little" ritual. If something requires a ritual, then it's probably bloody serious. Like releasing magic back into an unsuspecting Ireland, for instance.

Bres glanced sideways at me, a sly smile on his face. "Any last words?"

"Bite me."

"Ask again nicely when this is over, and I'll do whatever you like."

The smile I gave him showed too much too teeth to be friendly, but his grin just widened.

Pulling out his phone, he opened an app that showed four small black-and-white images. I squinted over his shoulder to see what he was looking at and recognised the museum that formed the public-facing facade for the Order's headquarters in one image. The picture next to it was a video feed of an empty corridor, while the third image showed a lounge area I'd passed through on my previous visit here.

The fourth video was the one that gave me greatest pause. The video feed came from inside Bannon's office, and showed the man himself sitting behind his desk, his attention fixed on something in front of him.

I realised suddenly that I didn't quite know what Bres's role was within the Order. Was he meant to have access to the CCTV system? And more to the point, was he meant to have access to a camera in Bannon's private office?

Before I had a chance to ask the question aloud, Bres grabbed my hand and tugged me across the road to the door of the building. "Come on. The museum is clear."

I had a moment to think again that I must be insane before Bres pushed open the heavy mahogany door and pulled me inside. Like the last time I'd been here, the reception area was empty. The two wing-backed chairs didn't look like they'd moved an inch, and I was pretty sure that the same pamphlets were fanned out on the small coffee table that rested between them.

Despite my reticence, I followed Bres through the frosted glass doors and into the museum beyond. A musty smell tickled my nose as I stepped into the narrow room, and I gave an involuntary shiver from the chill of the air conditioning. Glass cases bordered me on each side, spotlights highlighting their contents. Another time, I'd have been curious to explore the history stored in those cases. Now, I wanted nothing more than to turn around and run straight back out the door.

As Bres's CCTV footage suggested, there was no sign of anyone in the museum. Still, I felt uncomfortably exposed as we made our way towards the back of the room and the tapestry that I knew concealed the real entrance to the Order's headquarters.

We had almost reached the tapestry when a sound came from the far side of it. I froze.

The hidden door hissed opened, and before I knew what was happening, Bres shoved me behind a nearby cabinet. I swore silently and crouched low, my heart trying to hammer its way through my rib cage.

"What are you doing here?" a vaguely familiar voice demanded.

I covered my mouth to muffle my yelp of surprise.

"Bill," Bres smoothly addressed the museum curator. He leaned against the cabinet where I hid, blocking my view of the old man with the eye patch. "Good to see you too."

Bill harrumphed. "The boss doesn't have time for your nonsense right now. Surely, you should be off making yourself useful – somewhere else?"

"And miss the pleasure of seeing your welcoming face?"

I could almost hear the other man's scowl.

"Witty as ever." Bill sniffed and a moment later, clipped footsteps sounded.

I stiffened, afraid to even breathe as they passed me by. For the longest time, I stayed like that, terrified to move. When Bres tapped my shoulder to indicate the coast was clear, I honestly considered staying hidden. Only the fact my hiding place afforded little true cover should Bill return stopped me from giving into that temptation.

My knees protested as I rose and looked around warily. We were once again alone in the museum, and though my heart refused to calm to its normal rhythm, I loosed a breath.

I couldn't help but notice a tightness around Bres's eyes that hadn't been there before. It was clear from the brief interaction that there was no love lost between him and Bill, but was there more to it than that? The curator definitely hadn't made it sound like Bres was welcome.

"We don't have much time. Bannon will no doubt be informed that I'm here and will be expecting to see me."

Bres moved towards the tapestry without looking to see if I followed. He pushed it aside to reveal the keypad and the door beneath. Blocking the former from my view with his body, he punched in the code.

The door opened with a hiss, revealing an ominously empty corridor. Once I stepped through that final barrier, I would be wholly and completely at Bres's mercy. Did I really want to do this?

I had only a second to consider my decision as voices sounded from the reception area of the museum. My stomach flip-flopped with uncertainty, but I hurried past Bres into the waiting space. He let the tapestry fall back into place and pulled the door closed behind us, punctuating my decision as clearly as a death knell.

"Follow me," he said, his voice terse.

He led me through a series of winding corridors until we came to a stop outside what looked to be a fire exit. With a glance in each direction, he pushed the door open to reveal yet another corridor. Unlike the plush wine-coloured carpet and panelled walls currently surrounding us, a dusty concrete floor and exposed brick walls awaited us.

"Where are we?" I asked, following him through the opening.

"Servant's passages." Bres's jaw clenched almost imperceptibly in the dim lighting. "It wouldn't be good for the riff-raff to mix with the esteemed members of the Order more than necessary."

I wondered at the edge of bitterness in his tone, but said nothing as we continued on. After passing a number of grey doors, we finally stopped at one. It looked no different than the ones we'd passed, but Bres seemed sure of his choice. He held a finger to his lips, and my heart rate ratcheted up a few notches as he slowly eased the door open.

No sound came from whatever lay beyond, but I still had an urge to huddle back into the cold, hard safety of the service passage. Bres turned to me, and over his shoulder I caught sight of a familiar set of double mahogany doors – Bannon's office.

"Wait here. I'll get him out of the office so that you can sneak in and get the cauldron. You have the code I gave you?"

It was suddenly hard to swallow. I nodded.

"Okay. You have five minutes, then I'm going to cause a distraction. Make sure you're ready." He didn't wait for me to answer before he cleared the distance across the other corridor and rapped a jaunty tune on the mahogany doors.

The door to the service passage swung closed oh so slowly, and I had just enough time to hear Bannon snap, "What do you want?" before it shut fully and all sound grew muffled.

Heart racing and palms sweaty, I pressed my ear to the door. How the hell was I meant to know if the two men had left if all I could hear was the roar of adrenaline in my ears?

A moment later my question was answered. The muffled voices grew momentarily louder and then faded as they receded into the distance. I counted to ten Mississippi in my head, then before I could lose my nerve, I eased open the door.

The corridor was empty.

My knees nearly buckled with relief.

I scurried across the narrow space and through the mahogany doors into Bannon's office. It was as anally neat as I remembered. The black and silver accents gleamed under the cold white lighting, and not a speck of dust was visible on the rich wood furnishings. Did the man not shed skin cells at all?

Five minutes. That was how long I had before Bres returned to get me out of here. So, I put aside my thoughts on the head of the Order and shifted my attention to the bookcase behind Bannon's mahogany desk. It didn't take me long to find the book that concealed the keypad. My hand trembled as I reached out to type in the code Bres had made me memorise. A light flashed green and the bookcase began to move.

CHAPTER SEVENTEEN

A square room with stainless steel walls appeared before me. One complete side of the room was taken up by a computer setup that would be any hacker's wet dream, and I knew the right combination of keystrokes would reveal the treasures hidden behind those cold, imposing walls.

The last time I stood in this room, it had started a cascade of events that would change my life forever. Would it be the same this time?

Conscious of the seconds ticking away, I hurried over to the computer and brought up the log-on screen. *Dammit. What had Bres told me the password was?*

I chewed my lip as my brain suddenly lost the ability to form words, let alone form the complex sequence Bres had made me memorise before coming here. What would happen if I put in the wrong thing? Would it set off an alarm? Panic welled up inside me as I stood paralysed before the screen. I didn't have time for this; I needed to get my shit together.

Refusing to let fear get the better of me, I closed my eyes and forced my breathing to slow. By my third exhale, the tightness in my chest had eased marginally, and my thoughts cleared enough to recall the password. Before I could second-guess myself back into a state of panic, I typed the sequence and hit Enter.

No alarms went off, and no army of Order members burst into the room. The main screen simply loaded up, ready for me to use.

Bres had given me precise instructions on how to deactivate the security settings around the cauldron. He'd warned me not to get sidetracked, no matter how tempting it was. But when I spotted a folder on the screen titled "Guardian," all other thoughts fled my mind.

Did Bannon have information about me in there? About my ancestors?

My fingers twitched involuntarily. When would I ever get unrestricted access to the Order's database records again? Would it really hurt if I took a quick look?

As if in answer to my unspoken question, an alarm suddenly started blaring. I jerked my head towards the still open bookcase, my heart in my mouth. Had we been found out?

All desire to snoop was immediately forgotten, and I was spurred into action. I turned my attention back to the computer and followed Bres's instructions as quickly as I could physically make my fingers move across the keyboard. I hit the last key, and a low whirring sounded as the stainless steel panels slid back to reveal the glass cases behind them.

The wall closest to me showcased an assortment of artefacts, including broken sections of stone with strange markings and ancient looking scrolls. I ignored them, instead making my way to the far wall, where just three objects rested behind the glass. A spear, a straight sword, and a small cast iron cauldron.

The alarm continued to blare, grating on my last nerve as I unlocked the glass pane protecting them. As I reached inside to grab the cauldron, I found myself inexplicably drawn towards the sword. My fingers went so far as to graze the cool metal before I reined my wandering attention back in. What the hell was wrong with me?

I was surprised to find that the cauldron was a lot lighter than the black iron suggested. It wasn't large – roughly the size of a soccer ball – but as I lifted it down from its resting place, I suddenly realised I had no way of concealing it should someone spot me. Oh well, probably best to worry about getting out of Bannon's office before concerning myself with trivial little details like that...

Bres had said to wait in here until he came back for me, but the thoughts of staying in this room waiting to be found sent me into a cold sweat. So, gripping the cauldron tightly, I inched out of the hidden room and back into Bannon's office.

That's it, Aisling. One step at a time. You just have to get back to the service passage and make it through the museum without encountering Bannon, Bill, or any number of other Order members potentially in the building right now. Easy.

A nervous giggle escaped my lips. I clamped them shut. It was unlikely anyone might hear me with that infernal alarm going off, but best not to tempt fate.

I took a deep breath and gave my body a little shake. Time to focus.

Bres hadn't been able to give me too much actual detail on how the cauldron worked, so I wasn't sure if it was safe for me to use my magic while touching it. The thought of leaving this room without any additional protection was terrifying enough, however, that after only a short internal debate, I decided it was worth the risk.

I reached my senses outwards, feeling for the energy that surrounded me. It was rich and vibrant in a way that I hadn't yet encountered in the waking world, and I sucked in a breath. Presumably, the history held within these walls was adding to the strength of the magic, but was that all? An uneasy feeling skittered over me.

There would be time enough to examine the Order's power later, I reminded myself. For now, I focused on pulling the energy to me and letting it pool at my core. It wouldn't be enough to allow me to face off against an army of pissed off Order members, but I could use it to fuel my muscles and give me a vital burst of speed if needed.

Shoving the cauldron awkwardly under one arm, I reached for the door handle, in no way ready for this next step. Just as I touched it, the handle turned and the door swung open. I let a shriek and jumped back.

Bres stood in the doorway looking grim as he gave a quick scan of the space behind me, his gaze finally stopping on the cauldron in my hands. "We need to go."

"They know we're here?" I didn't think it was possible for my heart to race any faster than it already was, but apparently I was wrong.

He shook his head, impatiently beckoning for me to follow him. "Worse. Carmen is here."

My steps faltered. "What?"

"Carmen," he repeated, grabbing me by the elbow and tugging me across the hall and into the service passage. "She thinks the Order are harbouring you after I intervened in Dub's little kidnapping attempt. She's demanding Bannon hand you over, or she'll level the place."

"But Bannon doesn't know I'm here."

Bres's grin was brief but wicked. "Isn't the irony delicious."

I hurried after him as he carved a hasty path along the service passage, the only sound in my ears the blaring alarm and my own laboured breathing. The walls around us were hard and unforgiving. Could

Carmen really bring all of this down on us? The very thought quickened my pace and tightened my chest.

"Are the Order a match for her?" I asked hopefully.

Because if they were, and if casualties were likely to be minimal, then Carmen's appearance might be a useful distraction to aid our escape.

"No."

There was no question of doubt in Bres's clipped answer, and my fledgling spark of hope sputtered and died. I turned my attention inwards to the well of energy I'd gathered at my core, allowing myself to be comforted by it. I wasn't defenceless. I wasn't alone.

We came to a stop as the passage split into two paths, and Bres turned to me, tension clear in the sharp line of his jaw. "There's a fire exit up ahead. Bannon and Carmen were at the heart of the building last I saw them. I didn't stick around to find out if Bannon called for backup or gave the order for everyone to evacuate. Depending on how many of his people he's willing to sacrifice, we could be stumbling into the middle of a mass exodus when we leave here. Keep your head down and keep moving. With any luck, people will be too worried about their own asses to notice you."

Nervous butterflies cartwheeled around my stomach but I nodded, trying not to picture Bannon using the men and women here as human shields.

Silently, Bres turned left and headed to the end of the passage where we stopped at a fire door. He placed one hand on the door handle and held up three fingers on the other. He met my gaze with steady blue eyes, then one by one, counted down on his fingers.

Adrenaline roared through my veins as the third finger lowered, and he pushed open the door.

I'd prepared myself for the worst, for a hoard of stampeding Order members, all of whom would cease their fleeing to turn and point accusing fingers my way. I hadn't prepared myself for what actually awaited us.

The cold shock of air hit me as we stepped outside – and came face to face with Dub.

CHAPTER EIGHTEEN

Shadows swirled, forming a vortex that blocked our exit as surely as a solid wall would have. Dub's right eye gleamed in satisfaction, his left still a mangled mess of flesh from the jagged gash that ran across it. He smiled. "There you are."

The words slithered over me, freezing me to the spot.

Bres clearly had better survival instincts than me. He spun on his heel and shoved me back the way we'd come. "Run!"

My body responded even as my mind reeled, but Dub's shadows had other ideas. Darkness flowed past us and solidified into a terrifying black maw that filled the entire passage, forcing us to skid to a stop. I turned back, torn between facing Dub or his shadows. We were trapped.

"Any bright suggestions?" I cast a furtive glance at

Bres, praying he'd have an ace up his sleeve. His tight expression told me I was shit out of luck.

"Can you access the cauldron's power?"

I looked from him to the artefact tucked under my arm. Yes, the whole reason we'd come for it was to stop Dub and Carmen, but I hadn't planned on learning how to use the bloody thing on the job. *Dammit, why can't I be eased into life-or-death situations for once?*

Dub moved towards us, his steps slow and deliberate as he used his shadows to cage us into the narrow passage. Whatever little time we had to form a plan was swiftly dwindling, and unfortunately for us, I was our best chance.

Trying to think past the panic clouding my mind, I focused my senses on the cauldron. The power that emanated from it was similar enough to my own that I could almost taste the familiar tang of magic on my tongue. Despite that, it seemed distant, and I had no idea how to access it, let alone use it.

"Aisling, you might speed it up," Bres urged, stepping in front of me.

"I'm trying," I snapped, my concentration wavering as I fumbled with my hold on the magic.

"Try harder," Bres ground out.

He strode forward to meet Dub, who was almost within reaching distance now, and swung his fist in a right hook aimed at the other man's jaw. Shadows shot out and caught the strike before it could connect. They yanked Bres's arm to the side and drove him to his knees.

Bres's roar of pain sent a jolt of desperation through me; I had to help him.

Shifting the cauldron so that I gripped it tightly in both hands, I called on my siphoning magic. *Come on, dammit. Do something.*

Light flared at the centre of the artefact and strange symbols appeared around its edges. Heat built inside me, and there was an answering warmth from the cauldron, as if it recognised my power. Hope surged through me.

Just ahead of me in the passage, Bres clenched his jaw and got one foot under him followed by the other. The shadows pressed down on him, but he fought against them, rising to his feet.

Dub's hand locked around his throat, and he hauled Bres up until his toes scrambled at the floor for purchase.

"Bres," I screamed, almost dropping the cauldron as I reached out for him.

An explosion from somewhere deep within the building shook the ground beneath me, and my remaining hold on the cast iron pot slipped. As it hit the ground, I was dimly aware of Dub stumbling also. His grasp on Bres released as dust rained down in the passageway. My lungs spasmed with my next inhale and my eyes watered.

I crouched down, scrambling for Dagda's cauldron even as my vision blurred and my chest heaved with a coughing fit. Before I could rise, Bres was at my side. He gripped my elbow and pulled me to my feet.

"We have to get out of here. The place is going to crumble."

As if to punctuate his words, another explosion sent us both to our knees. Dust rained down on us, a jagged crack splitting the wall to my right. I forced myself to breathe shallowly so as not to start coughing again, but a band of fear tightened around my chest.

The space around us darkened, and I looked up to find Dub looming above me. Shadows writhed around him, and fury emanated from him in a force so powerful it burned like ice. I cowered away. But there was nowhere left to go.

A roar reverberated through the passage. The sound was so out of place that for a moment I thought my imagination was playing tricks on me. Then a huge brown wolf struck Dub from behind.

Dub crashed into the wall as teeth and claws flashed in a blur of lethal precision. I could do nothing other than gape as crimson gashes appeared across his chest and arms.

Shadows lashed out, attempting to contain the beast intent on carving Dub to pieces, but they had little effect. The wolf drove Dub backwards, forcing him to retreat until a narrow gap appeared in the passage, allowing a glimpse of the street on the far side of the fire exit.

Bres wasted no time in pushing me towards it. "Go!" he yelled.

My body responded on pure instinct, sprinting for

the sliver of daylight and the chance of safety that it represented.

The fight between Dub and the wolf spilled out from the building and into the narrow side street. Bres shoved me through the exit after them and we veered left, fleeing towards the main road just ahead. But as I reached it, I skidded to a stop.

"Oh god." I spun around, realisation slamming into me with dread as I was finally able to think straight again. "Pete."

I moved to turn back the way I'd come, but Bres grabbed my arm. "What the hell are you doing?"

I pulled against his grip, desperation driving me. "The wolf," I pleaded. "We have to help him."

Confusion creased Bres's brow and he looked at me like I'd lost my mind. "Are you insane? We need to get out of here. Now."

Any argument I could make was cut off as a car squealed to a stop beside us. Teagan shoved open the passenger door and leaned across from the driver's side.

"Get in," she ordered, then slammed her hand on the horn twice.

A responding growl came from further down the narrow side street followed by a bellow of rage.

I spun around, fear for Pete gripping my heart in a vice, but Bres blocked my view as he pushed me into the car and dived in after me. My protests were drowned out in a screech of tires as Teagan swung the car around in a manoeuvre worthy of the movies and aimed it down the side street.

She jammed on the brakes and slammed her hand on the horn again. This time she was rewarded by the sight of a huge brown wolf bounding for the car. The wolf leaped through the air, rebounded off the car's bonnet, and soared overhead and out of sight.

Apparently taking that as her cue to go, Teagan threw the car into reverse. Shadowy whips reached out for us as she sped back down the side street, spinning the car around once more. She hit the accelerator and we were off, speeding down the main road as car horns blared in our wake.

I glanced back, expecting to see Dub or his shadows following, but there was no sign of either. Slumping back into my seat, my whole body started to tremble. Had we made it? Were we safe?

Without a word, Bres leaned over and took the cauldron from my white-knuckled grip and placed it on the floor between us. He reached past me to pull the seat belt across my body and clip it into place, then did the same with his own.

"Where's Pete?" I demanded when I could get my body to stop shaking enough to form coherent words. Visions of his body lying defenceless somewhere flashed through my mind, and my stomach lurched at the thought of Dub finding it.

Teagan glanced at me through the rearview mirror, her eyes tight with tension. "He's safe. He'll meet us back at the apartment once he's ... feeling like himself again."

"No!" The word came out sharper than I'd intended and I hurried to clarify. "Dub will know to look there. We can't go back there."

Teagan nodded stiffly. "Where to, then?"

Bres answered before I could, his attention fixed out the window as he did. "You can go to my place. He doesn't know where it is."

There was a long silence as Teagan no doubt wondered, as I did, whether or not to trust him. Then she passed her phone back to me.

"Send Pete the address. Tell him to meet us there."

CHAPTER NINETEEN

I paced the length of Bres's penthouse apartment, ready to scream with each audible tick of the clock on the wall. Where the hell was Pete? Why wasn't he here yet?

Teagan looked only moderately less concerned than me as she sat in stony silence on Bres's beige sofa. Aside from her brief comment of reassurance in the car, she hadn't said anything further about Pete. With Bres still in earshot from the kitchen where he'd made himself busy, I could understand her reluctance to speak openly.

From what she *had* told me, my backup plan hadn't quite gone as I'd intended. Thinking about it now, I could see how sending Pete a message asking him to direct the Watchers to the Order's HQ if he didn't hear from me in an hour might be problematic. Naturally, he wasn't too inclined to sit idly by as I got myself into yet another stupid situation. Instead, he contacted Teagan and the two kicked into action.

One thing Teagan hadn't explained was why she'd encouraged him not to call in the Watchers straight away. I didn't miss the way her eyes turned stormy when she spoke of the group, but when I'd pressed, she'd quickly changed the subject. Only my concern for Pete kept my curiosity under wraps.

I was almost at the limit of my frayed nerves when there was finally a knock on the door. Before anyone else could react, I raced to it, yanked it open, and flung myself at Pete.

"Woah." He laughed, catching me mid-air and fixing his glasses that I'd knocked askew. "Good to see you too."

"I was so worried." I choked back a sob. Suddenly turning angry, I slapped his chest. "What did you think you were doing facing off with Dub like that? And where the hell have you been?"

He quirked an eyebrow and waited until I ran out of steam before answering. "It took a bit longer than usual to start feeling like myself again after burning so much energy." He gestured to the apartment behind me. "Any chance I can come in so we're not talking about this in the hall?"

Sheepishly, I stepped back to give him space to pass. As he did, I scanned him from head to toe for any sign of damage. He seemed to be favouring his left leg ever so slightly, but I couldn't quite say whether or not that was just my imagination.

Bres chose that moment to return to the living area. He gave Pete a nod that I assumed to be the male form of gushing gratitude, and handed him a bottle of beer.

Pete accepted it and settled himself on the sofa next to Teagan. He looked from me to Bres and then to Dagda's cauldron, sitting innocuously on one of the side tables. "Okay. Who's going to bring me up to speed?"

Dropping into his usual spot in the armchair, Bres swept out an arm to indicate the floor was mine.

Still too hyped to sit, I took that invitation literally and resumed my pacing. "Well, I guess you know already that Dub is alive. And I assume you know he has Carmen in tow?" I cast an accusing glare in Teagan's direction, unable to ignore the sting of hurt that flared up again at the reminder she'd kept something so vital from me.

"Actually, no." She met my gaze without flinching. "I guessed it might be the case, but the Watchers went radio silence on me after I returned from Wexford. Brian refused to tell me what was going on, and it was only when Pete reached out to me that I began to fully realise what was going on."

Hmm, maybe that explained her iciness towards the Watchers. I pushed the thought aside, recognising that we had more important things to worry about right now.

"Apparently, Dothar and Dain's deaths were enough to complete her resurrection. So, now Dub and Mommy Dearest both want my head on a platter."

"And this?" Teagan gestured towards the cauldron on the table next to her. "I'm guessing it's Dagda's cauldron, but I'm not sure why you wanted it enough to break into the Order. Or why you'd trust *him* to help you."

Bres simply grinned at the jab that was clearly directed at him and gave her a cheeky wink.

I wasn't surprised that Teagan knew the cauldron's name. Given her obsession with all things mythology, she could probably even tell me more about it than I already knew. Still, I took a moment to fill her in on what Bres had told me about the Tuatha artefact, and how we hoped to use it against Dub and Carmen.

"You can't seriously be thinking of going after them." She looked at me like I had officially lost what was left of my marbles, and truth be told, I wasn't sure she was wrong.

Pete jumped in before I had a chance to defend the decision, his tone calm and matter of fact despite the frown that marred his features. "Let's say you figure out how to get the cauldron working. What then? I mean yes, it would be good to disable their magic so they can't use it against you or anyone else. But what's to stop them from coming after you with a normal human weapon?"

And wasn't that the million-dollar question. I wasn't naive. There was every chance that even with their magic gone, I'd be no match for Dub or Carmen. I'd known that from the start of this. But there were only so many problems a girl could deal with at once.

My pacing slowed to a stop, and I turned to face him. "I don't know," I admitted. "I don't think I have it in me to kill them."

Sympathy shone in his brown eyes, and he nodded in understanding as I shrugged helplessly. "Okay. So, where does that leave us?"

Teagan gaped at him in disbelief. "Why are you encouraging her? This is insane. She'll get herself killed."

"She might. But if she doesn't do something, Dub and Carmen will certainly kill her. At least this way, we have the best chance against them."

"Woah. What do you mean 'we'?" I interjected.

Teagan shot me a glare that would have quieted even Satan himself. Her mouth set into a grim line of determination as she considered Pete's words. Finally, she nodded. "I'm in. What are our options?"

I opened my mouth and closed it again. Every part of me wanted to protest, to insist that there was no way they were putting themselves in danger for me again and therefore it wasn't for them to worry about the options. But I knew that would be hypocritical, and if I was truly being honest with myself, I didn't want to face this alone. I was terrified.

So, I focused on the practicalities. "We'll need some way to contain them, I guess. The Order are out of the question since they were the ones to bring the brothers here in the first place. And we can't exactly ring up the police and ask them to arrest two ancient magical beings." Reluctantly, I suggested, "What about the Watchers? Can we ask them to help?"

"I'm not sure we should trust them with this," Teagan said, not quite meeting anyone's eyes.

Again, I wondered at her change of heart towards the group. Part of me was happy her little Watcher bubble had burst, but I couldn't help wondering if there was more to it than the fact they'd kept Carmen's resurrection from her.

"We might have no choice," Pete pointed out, ever the pragmatist. "Brian is both a Garda and Watcher. If anyone has access to a means to contain Dub and Carmen, it's him."

He was right, of course. And damn if that didn't grate on me. The last person I wanted to ask for help was Brian, and if the tension in Teagan's shoulders was anything to go by, she was feeling the same. Still, unless we could come up with an alternative, we'd both have to swallow our pride.

"Let's park that for now." Maybe I could talk to Killian tonight and see if he had another suggestion? I needed to ask him about the cauldron anyway, since we hadn't yet figured out how to use the blood thing. "We need to think of a way to lure them out."

"Bait," Bres said simply.

I frowned at him. "What do you mean?"

"They want you. We offer them you."

"No way." A warning growl edged Pete's voice, and something shifted behind his eyes that sent a shiver down my spine.

Bres held up his hands in surrender. "Down boy. I don't mean we actually *give* them Aisling. We just let them believe she's offering the face-off they clearly want. Then when they arrive, we trap them and Aisling works her mojo with the cauldron."

I snorted. If only working my mojo was as simple as he made it sound. "And how exactly do you propose we trap them?"

"The stone circle at the Church of the Blessed Heart."

"The stone circle..." I thought about that, trying to follow his logic. "They're not descended from the Tuatha line, so how could they make it past the illusion spell to get to the ritual site? And even if they could, it's not like we can ask them to pretty please just stand there quietly while I drain them."

"I have magic dirt." Bres's eyes sparkled with mischief as he met mine, silently reminding me of a conversation we'd had what seemed like forever ago. I glared at him. "And surely there's something in that book of yours that can help you form a barrier around the stone circle."

"What book?" Teagan looked between me and Bres warily.

"I'll explain later," I assured her, an ache settling in my chest at the reminder of the distance that had grown between us. She should have been the first person I told about the book.

Pushing that thought away to be dealt with at another time, I turned my attention back to Bres.

"Okay, so to summarise, you're suggesting we lure them to the ritual site using me as bait. Somehow trap them in the stone circle so I can use the cauldron to siphon their powers, and voilà, no more psycho magic users trying to kill me and my friends?"

"Well, you could always jazz it up a bit by throwing in an epic lightsabre battle, but sure. That about sums it up."

I blew out a long breath, suddenly feeling wearier than I had words for. "How would we get a message – or your 'magic dirt' – to them?"

"We use the same channels the Order used to contact Dub and his brothers before – we send a message via Smith & Mercer."

Anger bristled through me at the mention of my old firm, but I nodded tightly.

"And why should we trust him?" Teagan demanded, looking with unbridled suspicion at Bres.

"Dub would've killed me multiple times over if it hadn't been for him," I answered quietly.

"That doesn't mean he won't turn on you again."

I met Bres's blue eyes as he watched me closely. "No. It doesn't."

CHAPTER TWENTY

I listened to Teagan's soft breathing in the bed next to me and marvelled at how peaceful she sounded. When the daylight had long since faded and it became clear we were all too exhausted to form coherent thought, Bres had offered up use of his spare room. Pete had insisted on taking the sofa, and bid us good-night with a pointed comment about being just outside the door if we needed him. More than once, I'd heard him move about, checking the locks on both the windows and doors.

Bres had been right about the book providing a barrier spell we could use. Together with Teagan, I'd scoured the pages for a viable option. I didn't ever remember seeing this particular spell on previous perusals, but the instructions were straightforward enough and, maybe more importantly, we were able to gather the ingredients with relative ease. I took it for the gift it was.

We still hadn't figured out how to activate the damn cauldron, but at least it seemed to be responding to my magic. Something told me we were missing one final key step, and I was hopeful that Killian might have the answer we needed. Of course, I'd kept that thought to myself – my trust for Bres only extended so far.

Despite the final snags that needed to be ironed out, our plan was starting to take shape. And with each detail that we settled on, my nerves grew. Lying in bed, staring at the unfamiliar ceiling, I couldn't help but wonder if I was handing my friends a death sentence.

It took a lot of tossing and turning before the room finally faded. The dreamscape formed around me, and I blinked against the sudden glare of daylight.

Aisling?" Killian was at my side in an instant, concern evident in his tone, though I doubted I looked any worse than the last time I'd been here.

"Hey." I gave him a tired smile and patted the ground next to me.

As he sat down, I couldn't help but notice that there were dark circles under his eyes and his jaw-length hair seemed more unkempt than normal.

Not quite ready to get straight into the heavy stuff, I gave his shoulder a little nudge. "How was your day?"

His lip quirked up at the side. "Oh, you know, long walks on the beach contemplating the meaning of life and coming up with solutions to world hunger."

I chuckled despite myself, and said conversationally, "I broke into the Order's headquarters and stole

Dagda's cauldron from them. Don't suppose you have an instruction manual for it?"

The silence stretched on so long that I glanced sideways at Killian. The muscle in his jaw was doing that funny twitching thing it did when I'd taken a few more years off his life with stress.

"You broke into the Order's HQ?"

"Mm-hmm."

"And stole an ancient artefact that they presumably had locked away under heavy security?"

"Security systems aren't much good when the other person has the code."

Yep, there was that funny little muscle tic again.

"Dare I ask what prompted this insane idea?"

I filled him in on the plan to use the cauldron against Dub and Carmen. His eyes turned stormy as I recounted the rough draft of our plan, but he didn't interrupt or argue against the obvious danger I'd be putting myself in.

"I don't like that he's involved in this," he said when I was finished.

"Bres has saved me a number of times now," I pointed out. "I'm not saying I trust him, but we do need him."

Killian didn't agree, but he also didn't argue. "The cauldron is keyed to Tuatha blood. Use your blood to activate it, and you'll be able to use your magic to amplify the cauldron's siphoning."

Okay, not the most appealing to have to shed my own blood, but simple enough.

"There's a problem, however," he continued.

Of course there was. My tentative little bubble of positivity burst.

"Our magic is an innate part of who we are. The cauldron can drain it and disable Dub and Carmen, but the effect will be temporary. It should be enough for you to contain them, but unless you can find a way to block their magic entirely, it will replenish over time."

My throat was suddenly very dry, and I had difficulty swallowing. "Are we talking years? Decades? Centuries?" I threw in that last once hopefully, but I could tell by Killian's expression that I was going to be disappointed.

"Days. Maybe weeks if you're lucky."

I dropped my head in my hands as a sinking feeling of helplessness pressed down on me. If their magic returned, it meant that anyone who helped us contain them would eventually be in danger. Even Brian, who was aware of the magical world, wouldn't have the means to hold back a power that ancient.

"Is there any way we can block their magic entirely? Without killing them," I clarified when he opened his mouth no doubt to suggest just that.

He closed his mouth again and turned his gaze from me. I could see an internal battle raging in his features, but I had no idea what he was thinking.

"There may be a way…"

"Tell me," I pressed, doing my best to tamp down the spark of hope that ignited in my chest.

He was quiet for the longest time, and there was obvious reluctance in his voice when he finally spoke. "I can trap them here."

"Here? In the dreamscape?"

Killian refused to look at me as he nodded. "It's part of the abilities of a Dreamwalker. We ... *I* can trap a person in their dreams."

The self-loathing in his tone was so palpable that I was overwhelmed by the urge to comfort him. But it was clear from the rigid way he held himself that he wouldn't welcome it, so I stuck to the practicalities.

"Would they need to be asleep?" We could probably get our hands on sleeping tablets to knock them out, but what would we do? Use blow darts to inject them while they were trapped inside the stone circle?

Killian closed his eyes for a brief moment before answering. "No. They'd just need to be unconscious so that I can access their subconscious thoughts."

I tried not to let my unease at that thought show on my face. It was obvious this was something Killian felt ashamed to be sharing with me. The last thing I wanted to do was make him feel bad for a gift he hadn't chosen; I knew all too well what that was like.

"What will happen if you bring them here?" Would it be dangerous for me to come here? What about Killian, trapped here with them both?

"You'll be safe."

Well, that told me nothing.

"What about you?"

"I'll be fine."

"But you'll be stuck here with –"

"All that matters is that you'll be safe." Killian turned to me, his dark eyes burning with determination. "Let me do this for you, Aisling. It's the only way I can make sure they can't hurt you again."

I opened my mouth to protest, but he reached out to touch my cheek, and the words died on my tongue. My breath caught. He leaned in and pressed his forehead against mine. And the dreamscape faded.

CHAPTER TWENTY-ONE

I awoke with the lingering sense of Killian's touch still on my skin. My heart beat erratically and an aching loss filled my chest. But I didn't have time to dwell on it. Not now.

A glance at my phone told me it was barely past dawn, and it was clear from the silence, interrupted only by soft breathing, that the others were all still asleep. As quietly as I could, I climbed from the bed and made my way to the kitchen where Dagda's cauldron rested on the marble island.

I settled on one of the high stools and stared at it for a long time. The knife block that sat within arm's reach on the counter offered me plenty of options for drawing blood, but the thought alone made my stomach queasy.

Stop being a wuss, I chastised myself, pulling out the largest knife in the set. If Tuatha blood was needed, I couldn't afford to be squeamish – not if I wanted to live.

With that thought firmly in mind, I closed my eyes and took a slow deep breath. I called my magic to the surface, and it instantly reached out to the cauldron's familiar energy.

The cauldron heated beneath my touch, and as they had before, symbols appeared around its edges. I didn't give myself time to think before jabbing my little finger with the tip of the knife. A bead of blood welled up and dripped into the centre of the cauldron. The final piece of the connection snapped into place with such force that I almost fell backwards off my stool.

In the living area, Pete leaped up off the sofa. "What the hell is that? Why do I smell blood?"

I couldn't speak, let alone answer Pete's question, so I held up a hand as Teagan and Bres came running out of the bedrooms to reassure them all that everything was okay.

Power skittered over my skin, and it took all my focus to hold the connection to the magic. A rainbow of colours spiralled out from the cauldron, forming tethers of power to each and every person in the room. All it would take was for me to reach out and pull, and I knew I'd be able to draw that power into the cauldron.

I took a shuddery inhale. God, so much power, and the Order had had it in their possession all this time. I didn't even want to think about what might have happened if they'd known how to use it.

Bres moved to my side, the glowing symbols casting his profile in an eerie glow. "You figured it out."

"Did you have any doubt?"

The look he turned my way burned with intensity. "Not for a moment."

"Okay." Teagan stepped between us, breaking our eye contact. "That's one problem solved. So, what do we do with the two ancient, uber-powerful beings once you've disabled them?"

I considered our options now that I had the added benefit of Killian's offer. Assuming we could rend them both unconscious, Killian would be able to trap Dub and Carmen in the dreamscape. But would that somehow include their physical bodies or just their minds so they wouldn't be able to use their magic? Dammit, why hadn't I asked more questions?

I shook my head and pushed away the irritation. It wasn't like I'd been trained for this shit. We just needed to make a decision and move on.

"I may have a way to contain Dub and Carmen, but to be on the safe side let's line up the Watchers for clean-up duty."

Bres leaned against the counter, quirking an eyebrow as he crossed his arms. "Care to share with the rest of us?"

Despite the seriousness of the situation, I couldn't contain my smirk of satisfaction at not being the one in the dark for a change. "I'm afraid you're just going to have to trust me, Hotboy85."

Pete snorted. "Hotboy85? Really?"

Bres scowled at us both.

"We'll need them unconscious for the containment to work." I looked at each of them hopefully. "I don't suppose any of you has a tranquilliser gun handy?"

The stunned silence that met my question pretty much summed up how bizarre this whole situation was.

Pete was the one who recovered from his surprise first. "I'm pretty sure the Watchers kept one close by during my early training sessions in case my wolf got out of hand. I may be able to ... borrow some of their equipment to help us."

"Is that a good idea?" Teagan asked, frowning. "We might want them for clean-up but if they get wind of what we're doing, we all know they'll come in and steamroll right over any plans we make."

"They won't even notice anything's missing," Pete assured her. "Besides, we're going to need some protective equipment in case you need to break out the high notes as a failsafe."

I didn't miss the flash of fear in Teagan's eyes, but she straightened her spine and nodded, determination turning her blue eyes steely.

"Okay," I said, the butterfly jig in my stomach turning into a rave. "If we're lucky, Dub and Carmen may have sustained some injuries when they attacked the Order's HQ yesterday. If we move tonight, we've a chance of catching them while they're still off balance." I looked at Bres. "Will that give you enough time to get the message to them?"

"Yes, but you don't want to give them too much

notice, or they'll have time to prepare their own ambush."

I'd thought of that already. Just like I'd thought of who I wanted at my back when the time came.

"That's why you'll stay behind," I said, meeting his gaze head on. "Once me, Pete, and Teagan get into position, I'll give you the signal to move."

Understanding darkened his gaze. "You don't want me at the church."

"I don't want any of us at the church," I countered. "This makes the most sense. It means we can delay sending the message to them until the last possible minute, and we have someone on standby to coordinate backup if shit goes south. Get your 'magic dirt' to Dub and then get in touch with Brian."

"What makes you think he'll listen to me? We're not exactly best buddies."

"I'm sure you can win him over with your charming personality."

Bres's grin didn't quite meet his eyes.

Sunset came far too soon for my liking. There was a disconcerting sense of déjà vu as we pulled to a stop in a narrow lay-by close to the Church of the Blessed Heart, and I couldn't help the shiver that ran down my spine.

Last time I was here, Dub and his brothers had kidnapped Pete to force me to come. This time I was here by choice. I could only pray there'd be less fatalities this time round.

My eyes flicked to the driver seat where Teagan had yet to release her death grip on the steering wheel. There was no sign of the purple glow that foreshadowed a coming death, but I took little comfort in that right now.

Logically I knew that her "gift" meant she'd no doubt foresee my end – should that be the outcome – no matter where she was at the time. Still, it seemed cruel to bring her here to witness it first hand. Yes, her skills and the early warning might be enough to turn the tide, but I'd accused the Watchers of trying to weaponize her. Did this make me any better?

Unclipping his seatbelt, Pete grabbed the black rucksack from the back seat next to him and climbed out of the car. He'd been quiet the whole drive here, no doubt reliving his own bad memories, but his jaw was fixed in a determined line as he waited for us to follow. I gave Teagan a weak smile and picked Dagda's cauldron up from the footwell of the car. Together, we climbed out after him.

As soon as I stepped away from the safety of the car, I became aware of the eerie silence that filled the space. With the icy bite to the air and the late hour, I wasn't surprised by the lack of tourists. I'd pretty much counted on the site being closed off to visitors given the damage Bres had warned me about. I still would've expected some signs of life, however.

With a growing sense of trepidation, we made our

way to the two large oak trees that marked the entrance to the Church of the Blessed Heart grounds. My steps faltered as they came into view and Teagan hissed in a breath. At my side, Pete's snarl of anger was so animalistic that I actually did a double take to make sure he hadn't freed his wolf when I wasn't looking.

The beautiful trees that had stood strong for centuries on the grounds were now shadows of their former selves. Their thick trunks were grey and crumbling, and an insidious black rot crept up from the roots towards a jagged crack that ran through the centre of the trees. And that was just the beginning of the destruction as we continued up the gravel path towards the graveyard.

Though Bres had sent me photos of the devastation caused by Carmen's poisonous magic, seeing it first hand almost took my breath away. Throughout the graveyard, many of the old tombstones had tumbled to the ground, the earth around them too parched and crumbling to support their weight any longer. The natural foliage that had thrived here previously was now little more than rotten mulch. And worse still was the gaping void of energy that surrounded the place. It was as if all the life had been drained away.

In the midst of it all, I was relieved to see the ruins of the church still standing strong. The jagged outline loomed against the backdrop of the darkening sky, a symbol of defiance that gave me strength when hopelessness threatened to overwhelm me. And just beyond that, over the stone boundary wall, was the unnaturally perfect green field that I now knew to be little more than an illusion. Hidden behind that illusion was the stone circle that would help us end this.

I turned to Pete, trying not to let the nerves show on my face as I gestured to his rucksack. "Want to show us what you got?"

He dropped the bag to the ground and opened it. "The lady requested a tranq gun?" He held up what looked like a small pistol and grinned. Placing it down next to the bag, he reached in again. This time he held up a pair of small ear-plugs to me. "I considered taking the soundproof headphones they use in the observation room but figured it might be too dangerous for us not to hear what's going on around us."

I took the ear-plugs from him and eyed them sceptically.

"They should muffle sound enough that if Teagan has to break out the high notes, it will give us time to flip this switch here" – he pointed to a tiny switch I'd almost missed on the side of the outer shell – "and activate the soundproof mode."

I didn't want to think how much trouble we'd be in if that needed to be our failsafe plan, but it was better than nothing. So, rather than worrying about the future potential of my brains to leak out of my head, I gestured for him to continue.

Placing a second pair of ear-plugs aside for himself, he proceeded to lay out a number of other odd-looking objects for us to see. "Obviously, we want to engage with Dub or Carmen as little as possible, but just in case, I got a taser, some smoke bombs, and a mini crossbow. Oh, and here." He held a small knife out to me. "For the blood."

I took it with a grimace.

Eyeing the selection before us, Teagan bent down and picked up the mini crossbow. She turned it over in her hands and checked the mechanism. "Looks like we've got ourselves a party."

CHAPTER TWENTY-TWO

It didn't take us long to prepare everything we needed. I wasn't sure whether to be grateful that the waiting was over or terrified of what came next. The temptation to run and hide was almost impossible to ignore, but as I stood with Teagan, Pete already having left to find cover near the stone circle, I knew that wasn't an option.

"Are you sure I can't convince you to at least watch from the car?" I tried one last time.

Teagan gave me a wry smile and squeezed my hand. "I need to be here. If there's any chance I can make a difference to the outcome... Well, there's no way I'm letting you hog all the glory."

My laugh caught on a sob at the end. "No. We can't be having that."

A heavy silence fell between us. Throat burning, I pulled her into a tight hug. She gave me a quick squeeze, then stepped back, her expression fiercer than I'd ever seen.

"You better make it out of this in one piece, Aisling. Don't make me see my best friend's death."

With nothing to say that could top that guilt trip, I fixed the ear-plugs in my ears, carefully pocketed the small knife Pete had left me, and carried Dagda's cauldron over to Betty Anne's grave.

I'd chosen the spot to ensure I had a clear line of sight to the field beyond the church grounds. I wasn't sure what limitations the cauldron's magic had, but I wanted to minimise physical impediments between me and my target. In an odd way, it also gave me comfort to think that maybe my ancestor would be looking down on me as we made our stand, though I had no idea if any trace of her still resided in this place.

By the time I settled myself at the lifeless carcass of the cherry blossom tree and lay the cauldron and a small knife on the ground next to me, Teagan had disappeared into the ruins of the old church out of sight. Pete had also somehow managed to camouflage himself in an all but empty field, hopefully keeping well out of sight of our expected guests. Regardless of what fun little toys he had in that rucksack, I was under no illusion that he'd be a match for Dub and Carmen should they spot him.

With everyone in place, there were no more excuses to delay. Guess it was time to get this show on the road. Ignoring the tremble of my hands, I pulled out my mobile and hit send on my message to Bres.

Do it.

Then I sat down to wait.

I wrapped my hands around the cauldron like I would a mug of hot chocolate on a cold day as I counted the minutes ticking away. The chill that permeated my bones at this moment had little to do with the weather, but still I took comfort from the feel of the hard iron beneath my fingers.

When my phone finally buzzed, my heart froze in my chest. Feeling somewhat nauseous, I looked down at Bres's message.

Incoming.

Oh god, we were actually doing this. What the hell had I been thinking?

Something moved near the church ruins, and as I squinted in the darkness, a swirling mass detached itself from the shadows. My fingers dug into the edges of the cauldron and it was all I could do not to bolt.

I watched as the storm of shadows made its way towards the field and the boundary of the illusion spell that blocked the stone circle from sight. Try as I might, I couldn't make out any detail within the void of darkness. Dub was clearly making sure his mother was well protected.

Anticipation tightened my chest and a somewhat numb, somewhat hysterical, part of my brain wondered if it would be an issue if I got sick into the cauldron. Of course, I wasn't going to do that because I wasn't the same weak, unprepared Guardian Dub and his brothers lured here last time... At least I hoped I wasn't.

It was an effort to breathe normally, but I forced myself to focus on the well of power pooled at my core. I didn't dare call on my magic or the magic of the cauldron yet, lest it attract Dub and Carmen's attention before they were safely trapped within the stone circle. Still, I took comfort from its closeness.

Movement to the left of the swirling shadows caught my eye, and my breath caught as I realised that Pete was on the move.

What was he doing? It wasn't time yet. They'd see him.

Panic clawed its way up my throat, and I had to cover my mouth to stop myself from calling out to him in warning. Why hadn't we thought of bringing some comms equipment, dammit? Yes, it would have left us more exposed to Teagan's powers, but if Pete got himself killed, none of that would matter.

"What are you doing?" I whispered, gripping the edge of the cauldron so tight that the metal bit into my hands.

"Following his instincts, I should think. It's a pity yours aren't so finely tuned."

The voice that came from directly behind me turned the blood in my veins to ice. Slowly, as if delaying the inevitable would change the outcome, I turned.

A woman towered over me. At least six and a half feet tall, she was broad shouldered and all lean muscle.

Long black hair flowed to her waist, and her eyes... oh god, those eyes.

"Carmen." The name left my lips on an exhale as if I'd been physically struck in the gut. Fear tightened every muscle in my body.

She smiled. "Stupid girl. Did you think we would not know what it was you stole from the Order? Did you really think my son would not recognise such a powerful artefact?"

Horror filled me and I tightened my hold on the cauldron. In truth, no. It hadn't even occurred to me that Dub might have spotted the artefact during our encounter at the Order. I'd been so shocked and relieved to make it out of there in one piece that I hadn't even considered the possibility that we'd given away our intentions.

Bile rose up in my throat and I swallowed hard. Could I drain her before she reached me? I doubted it. Even if the cauldron's magic had been ready and waiting to go, it would take time to fully work. And then there was Dub to worry about.

The reminder of a second deadly threat was enough for me to risk a glance back to the field where Pete was. I caught the exact moment that the whirling vortex of shadows stopped moving – just at the edge of the boundary line. The darkness solidified into Dub's familiar form. And he turned to face Pete.

That moment of distraction was one I couldn't afford.

Carmen held out her hand and a blast of air drove

me backwards, wrenching the cauldron from my grip. I hit the ground with a jarring thud, and pain radiated through my back.

She contorted her fingers into a claw shape and black veins spiralled up her arms. With a whispered word, the ground around me split. Black veins shot up from the barren earth and wrapped around my legs and arms.

I yanked against the restraints, panic driving me to flood my muscles with magic and demand that they be stronger, that they break these unnatural bonds. The vines only tightened furthered.

Desperation drove me on, but the well of energy that I was drawing upon was fatiguing rapidly. Where Carmen had somehow been able to pull magic from the barren earth, I could sense no energy to draw from, and I'd almost burned through the reserves I'd come with.

A strange glow lit the darkness, and I tore my attention from my struggles to look at Carmen, who was strolling towards me, her dark eyes gleaming. She held Dagda's cauldron in her hands, the black veins creeping from her arms up the side of her face as she spoke indecipherable words. Symbols glowed all around the cauldron's edge, and power pulsed to the rhythm of her words.

I began to struggle in earnest.

CHAPTER TWENTY-THREE

Leisurely, as if she had all the time in the world, Carmen bent to pick up the small knife I'd placed on the ground, ready for use. She turned it from side to side, the moonlight glinting off the blade as she did. Then she looked at me and smiled.

My lungs forgot how to expand.

I pulled on every ounce of power I could dredge up, short of draining my own life force, in my desperate attempt to put even an inch more space between us. It wasn't enough.

Carmen's vines tightened painfully as she crouched down next to me, and oh so slowly, ran the edge of the knife down my arm. Blood welled up and coated the blade. Her eyes gleaming like black obsidian, she raised it up and licked one side of the knife. Then she plunged the blade with the remainder of the blood into the cauldron.

Time hung suspended for what seemed like an

eternity. Then the cauldron's full power flared to life. It sucked all the oxygen molecules from the air, drawing them in, then expelling them in a whoosh of energy that left me breathless.

Satisfaction twisted Carmen's lips into a cruel sneer as she stood. "You are an embarrassment to your bloodline. You are weak. It is an insult that my sons fell to you."

A piercing pain shot through the centre of my core. I gasped and would have clutched my hands to my midsection had I been free to do so. But when I looked down, there was no blood and no wound.

The sensation intensified and the world shifted around me. Colours became muted and the buzz of energy that I'd only just grown used to feeling dimmed. It was as if the magic was slowly being sucked from the world.

Only it wasn't being sucked from the world. It was being sucked from me.

Horror filled me as I realised what was happening. *No! She can't have it. She can't have my magic.*

I dug my fingers into the crumbling earth beneath me and focused only on the anger, pushing away the crushing sense of hopeless despair that pressed down on me. I bared my teeth.

"You're wrong. Your sons were the ones who were weak. They destroyed lives so that they could play God. Well, look how that worked out for them."

Carmen let an inhuman screech and lashed out at

me. A trail of fire blazed across my cheek as she struck me, and my vision darkened for a moment.

Shifting her grip on the cauldron, she held out a black-veined hand towards me. The vines binding me fell away, but before I could so much as flex an aching muscle, an invisible force hauled me upright. I hung in the air immobile and powerless.

"I'll show you what a god truly looks like," she snarled, locking her hand around my throat in a crushing grip. Her eyes flashed golden and the world around us shifted.

When everything came into focus again, what remained of the cherry blossom tree was gone. We were no longer at Betty Anne's grave, but rather smack bang in the middle of the unnaturally green field, where mere feet from us Dub and Pete were engaged in a lethal dance that from initial glance at least, neither seemed to be winning.

Carmen released her hold on me and I crumpled to the ground, my stomach roiling as if I'd just done thirty minutes straight on the Waltzer at a local fairground. What the hell had happened? I shook my head, trying to clear the fog of confusion, and instinctively reached for my magic. There was nothing. Just a horrible emptiness.

Pete let a vicious snarl as he spotted me, his movements almost a blur as he dodged one of Dub's shadowy tendrils. Despite the obvious danger he was in, he was showing immense control in not releasing his wolf. Still, his movements appeared almost animalistic, and I could've sworn his eyes glowed in the dim light.

I scanned the area for any sign of Pete's rucksack, terrifyingly aware of how useless I was to help without my magic. It lay on the ground about twenty feet away from me, and I could see a number of the smoke bombs scattered around it.

Carmen was too close to me; there was no way I'd make it to the bag or the smoke bombs before she stopped me. But my eyes fell on a dark object, almost hidden within the grass not far from me. The tranq gun.

"Stop playing with the mutt," Carmen snapped, drawing my attention back to her as she placed the cauldron on the ground at her feet. "Finish him and be done with it."

At her command, a whip of shadows shot out from either side of Dub and struck Pete. They sent him careening through the air and he struck the ground with a bang. He lay there unmoving.

I screamed and scrambled to his side, desperately praying for him to be all right.

Conscious of the double threat now at our backs, I flung myself over Pete's body. Without my magic, I felt vulnerable in a way I hadn't in a long time. But I was determined to keep him from further harm in whatever way I could. Where the hell was Teagan? If ever we needed to press the big red button, it was now.

Pete's eyes flashed open, and I had to smother my gasp of surprise as he held a finger to his lips. Relief coursed through me, quickly followed by confusion as I tried to scan his huddled form for any sign of damage. Was he hurt?

Slowly, in a clear attempt not to attract attention, he gestured towards his pocket nearest me. I frowned but reached my hand inside. I pulled out a small black object – the taser he'd borrowed from the Watchers.

Pete flicked his eyes up, gesturing behind me just as Carmen ordered, "Fetch the Guardian. Bring me to the place where she killed my sons. We will spill her blood this night."

Fear threatened to lock my muscles up tight, but I fought against the instinct. I slowed my breathing as much as I could and listened carefully for Dub's approach. I waited until the last possible moment, until my skin crawled with the nearness of him.

Then I twisted, lunged upwards, and tased the fucker in the balls.

Dub collapsed to the ground, his whole body spasming. The look of pure agony on his face filled me with a perverse sort of pleasure that I wasn't the least bit apologetic for. Good luck trying to procreate now!

Pete took the moment of distraction to lunge for the tranq gun that lay in the grass a few feet to his left. He fired off a shot at Carmen, but she deflected with a simple flick of her wrist.

Whether she was angered more by Pete's attack or by me hurting yet another of her children, I wasn't sure, but she began chanting and power crackled in the air. A fierce wind whipped up, blowing my hair into my eyes and almost knocking me from my feet.

Pete was at my side in an instant, bracing me against the force of the wind. I was about to demand he get the hell out of there when movement behind Carmen caught my attention.

Carmen's words increased in pitch and the grass around her started to wither and die. The black veins now covered almost every visible surface of her, and they undulated beneath her skin. Her eyes flooded with black.

The wind whipped at us, slicing at our skin as if it were made up of thousands of tiny daggers. Tears stung my eyes and I blinked furiously to clear my vision as Carmen raised her arms to the sky.

A crossbow arrow shot out of the darkness and pierced her in the side. She doubled over, her words cutting off abruptly.

"Uh-uh. No you don't." Teagan stepped out of the shadows, reloading the mini crossbow as she moved. With the crossbow aimed at Carmen, she bent to pick up Dagda's cauldron.

Carmen snarled at her as she backed slowly away, her aim never once wavering despite the roaring wind that continued in a frenzy around us.

Teagan joined me and Pete with a wary glance at Dub, who was already rising to his feet, the taser battery apparently running out. "Don't suppose you still have that knife?"

I shook my head as we all backed further away.

"What do you need?" Pete flashed his right hand. The nails had somehow lengthened and looked terrifyingly sharp.

"Blood." Teagan held her left arm out to him as she kept hold of the crossbow in her right hand. "Yours too."

He didn't question her, just sliced his nails across her arm in a shallow gash before doing the same to his own forearm.

As they were doing this, Dub rose to his full height. He let a furious roar and shadows flowed from his open mouth to fill the night above him.

"If you have a plan, you might want to make it quick," I urged, my mouth going dry as the vortex of darkness expanded and moved towards us.

"We're all Tuatha." Teagan held her arm over the cauldron, letting her blood drip down to join mine.

Carmen straightened and wrenched the arrow from her side. She flung it away and stalked towards us.

Power pulsed from the cauldron and Pete's eyes lit with understanding. He hurriedly followed Teagan's example and forced a few drops of his blood to fall. "Let's show them exactly what that means."

The three of us gripped the cauldron as our blood combined at the bottom. And as one we began to chant the words that flowed through us on the current of magic.

CHAPTER TWENTY-FOUR

Even with my own magic gone and my senses dulled, the power building was enough to take my breath away. Dub and Carmen jerked back as the magic of the cauldron was focused on them, but they recovered from their shock far too quickly. With gritted teeth and murder in their eyes, they came for us.

The distance between us lessened with every heart-beat, and I knew there was no way we'd be able to drain them both before they could reach us.

Teagan clearly had come to the same realisation. Her eyes flicked from me and Pete to Carmen and Dub. I saw fear darken her blue eyes, then I saw the moment they hardened to a determined steel.

She opened her mouth and screamed.

Terror washed over me. In all the chaos, I hadn't had a chance to switch my ear-plugs to noise cancelling. There was no way I could release my hold on the cauldron to do it now – not while Dub and

Carmen still stood – which meant I'd be as susceptible to Teagan's magic as they were. Oddly, the thought filled me with a sense of acceptance. I didn't want to die, but if that was only way we could stop them, then so be it.

Only the skull-shattering pain never came. In fact, the wind that had been whipping around us moments before seemed to suddenly just disappear. There was no sound at all.

I blinked in confusion and looked around. A strange shimmering filled the air, surrounding the three of us and the cauldron. Teagan's mouth was wide open, frozen in a death scream, but it was soundless, as if we'd somehow stepped into an old silent movie.

On the far side of the shimmering sphere, Dub and Carmen were still visible, less than five feet from us now. As the cauldron's siphoning took hold, the swirling mass of darkness that had been born of Dub's shadows was dissipating, and the black veins covering Carmen's skin appeared to be fading. They didn't stop coming for us, however. And whatever Teagan's scream was doing, it didn't seem to be having an effect on them either.

Carmen reached the shimmering barrier first.

I was about to scream at my friends to run, when she lunged for me. One minute, she was mid-air, striking the barrier, the next she was on her knees, head thrown back in agony as she clutched her ears.

Dub moved as his mother fell. He flung out his hands as if to send whips of shadows our way, but the darkness was no longer his to control. He bellowed in rage and ran for us. He, too, ended up on the ground, clutching his head as blood streamed from his nose.

I stared at them both in shock, then back to Teagan. Sweat was running down the side of her face, and her body was shaking with the effort of whatever magic she was controlling. We had to end this now.

Looking around for any sign of the tranq gun Pete had dropped, I spotted it only a couple of feet from me. On the far side of the barrier.

Shit. What would happen if I touched the barrier? Would I be able to function long enough to put a dart in both Dub and Carmen? There was no way we'd get this chance to stop them again. It was a risk I had to take.

With one final look at the friends who had stood by me through all this insanity, I released my hold on the cauldron and dived for the gun. Pain shot through me as I struck the barrier, and every nerve in my body felt like it was short-circuiting. I screamed in agony, but pressed forward. I had to end this.

The suddenly, the resistance was gone.

I was dimly aware of Teagan calling my name, and it was with a strange sense of detachment that my fingers wrapped around the cold metal of the tranq gun. Guided purely by instinct, I swung around and fired two shots just as Dub and Carmen both released their grip on their bleeding ears.

The darts struck them in the centre of the chest.

For a moment, nothing happened. Then their eyes

fluttered and they collapsed to the ground. I followed straight after, my knees buckling with overwhelming relief.

Pete was there a moment later, checking me for signs of injury and supporting me as I sat back in the grass. "Aisling? Are you okay? Are you hurt?"

I shook my head weakly. "Teagan?"

"I'm okay," she called from behind me, exhaustion lacing her words.

I twisted around to see for myself, and sure enough, she too had sunk to the ground and was sitting with her arms wrapped around the still glowing cauldron. The shimmering barrier was nowhere to be seen, and whether Teagan had released the magic intentionally or out of pure exhaustion, I was grateful.

"We did it," I whispered with a numb sense of disbelief.

"And I didn't make your brains explode." Teagan gave me most half-hearted thumbs up ever, and I couldn't help the hysterical giggle that slipped past my lips.

I was going to have to quiz her on that funky shimmering forcefield later, but for now I was just glad to be alive and with my brains intact. Even if the hollow emptiness at my core did feel like a vital part of me was missing.

"Should we check that they're actually unconscious?" Pete asked, eyeing Dub and Carmen warily.

"Probably." I sighed. "Anyone see a stick I can poke them with?"

Before anyone could answer, there was a sound of a car approaching in the distance. All of us turned to look, though the road was too far from the field for us to see anything other than the dim glow of headlights.

"Guess the clean-up crew is here." Pete ran his hand through his messy hair and stood.

Slowly, on account of my legs apparently being replaced by jelly, I got to my feet too. It wouldn't be long before the Watchers reached us, and it was only as we stood here now with two unconscious homicidal maniacs that I realised there was a detail we'd over-looked in our planning.

"What should we do with the cauldron?" I asked.

While I was okay with the Watchers taking Dub and Carmen's bodies, that was only because I was confident Killian would keep their consciousness firmly under lock and key. Dagda's cauldron, on the other hand, was currently brimming with power – mine as well as Dub and Carmen's. What might the Watchers do if they had access to the siphoned magic?

Apparently, I wasn't the only one concerned by that thought. Pete and Teagan both frowned and Teagan lifted the cauldron up, gesturing for me to take it.

"Maybe hide it somewhere until they've gone," she suggested. "We can always give it to them later, once we've had a chance to think about it properly."

I nodded and took it from her. The stone circle was the closest option for it, hidden as it was from sight beyond the boundaries of the illusion spell. Of course, the Watchers were of Tuatha descent too, so now that magic had returned, there was every chance they could cross the spell's boundary. If we didn't give them a reason to look there, maybe it would be fine as a temporary option.

My time for hemming and hawing was cut short as I heard the muffled sound of footsteps approaching. Stone circle, it was.

I turned to make my way towards the spot where the perfect green grass appeared just slightly less than perfect, but a voice I'd never expected to hear stopped me in my tracks.

"How kind of you to top that up for us."

CHAPTER TWENTY-FIVE

I turned to find Declan Bannon striding towards me in his perfectly tailored Armani suit. Bill, the museum curator, flanked him on his left, looking suspiciously like he was here to bury our bodies despite the fact he, too, was dressed in a pristine suit. And on the right was Bres.

He refused to meet my gaze as the group closed the gap with us. Instinctively, I clutched the cauldron to me, but when I heard more car doors closing in the distance, I knew it was pointless.

"Motherfucker," Teagan hissed, standing as Pete, too, let a low warning growl.

Bannon didn't so much as blink in their direction as he came to a stop about ten feet from us. He did, however, raise an eyebrow at the two unconscious bodies. "Interesting."

"What do you want?" I asked as calmly as I could.

Maybe if we were lucky, they'd just popped out for an evening stroll and would be on their way?

"Why, I would like my property returned, Ms. O'Meara."

"The cauldron belongs to the Tuatha," Teagan countered, moving to my side. "You're not Tuatha."

Bannon pretended to consider her point for a moment before fixing her with a steely smile. "That is a fair point."

He turned to Bres, who was standing with his gaze fixed firmly ahead and expression unreadable. "Bres, please make that unfortunate heritage of yours useful and go retrieve the cauldron from Ms. O'Meara."

Bres's shoulders tensed almost imperceptibly, but he stepped forward. Only when he drew close to me did he finally meet my gaze. I saw my own frustration and helplessness mirrored back at me.

"I thought we had an understanding," I said quietly as he reached to take Dagda's cauldron from my hands.

Pete moved to stop him, but I put a hand on his chest as I spotted three other men heading through the darkness towards us, the unmistakeable silhouette of guns in their hands. I had a feeling this was a fight we wouldn't win.

Bres looked at the hand I'd used to stay Pete's movements and back to me. "You really should be careful who you trust."

He gave me that familiar cocky grin, but his eyes were beseeching. "Let me take this off your hands, and you can go home and put your feet up with a good book."

Something sparked inside me at his words. A tenuous hope that maybe – just maybe – things weren't as black and white as they seemed. Still, I couldn't help my anger as I watched him carry the uber-powerful cauldron back to Bannon. Any harm they did with it would be my fault, maybe even caused by my own magic. The thought made me sick to my stomach.

Bannon acknowledged his return with little more than a flick of the eyes. "Good to see you can be of use sometimes."

I didn't miss the ways Bres's steps faltered ever so slightly, but he simply smirked at the head of the Order. "Say please, and I might even be helpful more often."

A pointed silence was the only response as Bannon and Bill both turned and began to make their way back to the church, clearly unconcerned with any possibility of attack while their backs were turned. Bres gave me one final look, then turned to follow.

Wrapping my arms around myself, I tried to hold back the shivers that threatened to wrack my body as I watched them go. The three remaining Order members kept their guns trained on us until the others were out of sight. I didn't have the energy to worry about them shooting us. I was so completely and utterly spent.

Had it all been for nothing? Yes, Dub and Carmen

were no longer waiting in the shadows to kill me, but the Order had the cauldron. And they had my magic.

Eventually, the three with the guns retreated. There was no word of warning to keep our mouths shut, no threats to our well-being. The Order couldn't have made it any clearer how much of a threat they viewed us as.

I slumped to the ground, dejected. "What do we do now?" I whispered, no longer able to hold back the tears that burned my eyes.

Teagan shuffled to my side and wrapped an arm around me. "We go home."

I was exhausted. By the time we dropped Pete home and headed back to the apartment, I was ready to sleep for a decade. But I knew there'd be no sleep for me. Not with Bres's words echoing in my head.

As Teagan pulled into the underground car park, a jolt of fear ran through me and I tensed in my seat.

Dub is gone, I reminded myself. *He can't hurt you now.*

At least I hoped he couldn't.

Teagan glanced sideways at me, clearly noticing my reaction. "Did you see the way Brian's face went that funny shade of purple when he arrived for cleanup?"

As she no doubt had intended, I snickered.

Since Bannon and his goons hadn't had the decency to help us deal with Dub and Carmen's unconscious bodies before they left, we'd had to return to plan A and call the Watchers. In truth, it was probably for the best since I didn't trust the Order to keep custody of a stuffed animal, let alone two life-sized homicidal maniac dolls. I thought Brian was going to have an apoplexy when I gave him a heavily redacted version of events over the phone, but at least he'd shown up. Of course, we were now under orders to present ourselves at Watchers HQ tomorrow under threat of being arrested for assault if we failed to show.

"We're going to get such a bollocking tomorrow." I sighed and leaned my head back against the headrest. "I don't even know where to start with a plausible explanation that won't require us to tell the Watchers everything."

Teagan reached over and squeezed my hand. "We'll figure it out. Together."

As we climbed out of the car, I looked at her. "Teagan? How did you learn to do that funky barrier thing? You've never mentioned that before."

Her smile was tired, but something glimmered in her eyes that looked suspiciously like pride. "Your book told me how. Back at Bres's when we were looking for a barrier spell. I didn't say anything because I wasn't sure it would work. I wasn't sure my power was capable of anything that might actually save a life rather than..."

I nodded in understanding as she trailed off. It was scary to feel like your innate ability was only capable of destruction, scary to think what it might say about you.

We fell silent as we made our way to the lift and up

the third floor. Only when she'd unlocked the door and we'd switched on every light possible did Teagan turn to me again, looking somewhat uncertain.

"There was something else in the book too."

"Oh?"

"A name. I think ... I think it might be the name of someone who can help me with all of this."

I considered that for a moment. Somehow the book always seemed to know what I needed. Nobody could deny that Teagan needed someone to help her navigate her banshee ability in a safe and healthy way. Had the book given her the answer to that?

Too tired to even figure out how that might be possible, I decided to trust whatever magic had helped us this far.

"We should look into that."

Something in her seemed to relax at my words. She gave me a quick hug and headed for her bedroom.

The smart thing for me to do would be to follow suit, but instead I collapsed onto the sofa, reached into my bag, and pulled out the book that thankfully was still in my possession, even if the cauldron – and my magic – wasn't.

I tried to ignore the unnatural void at my centre where my magic normally was. I had no idea when it had become such a vital part of me, but now that it was gone, I felt lost. Killian had said it would return. But what if it didn't? And what could the Order do with my power now they had access to it?

Since that line of thinking would only drive me

crazy, I pushed the thought away and flipped open the book.

The familiar note from my ancestors covered the first page as it always did. I ran my fingers over the words tenderly. "Thank you for helping her. And for helping me."

I continued on, searching.

Bres said the Order needed to gather power to complete the Claiming. Did the cauldron give them that power, or did they need more still?

As before, I found no reference to the Claiming other than in the note at the front. But about ten pages in, I stopped.

Conduits of power.

My whole body tensed as I scanned the text. While it didn't reference Dagda's cauldron specifically, it talked of artefacts and magical objects that could be used to store power to be used at a later time. While a magical battery pack sounded quite useful, I didn't miss the relevance to my current situation. Or the undercurrent of warning that ran through the text.

It is the intent of the user alone that determines where a conduit of power presents on a scale from good to evil. Be aware that the line between the two can often become blurred if we are not careful.

An prickling foreboding settled over me as I continued reading.

CHAPTER TWENTY-SIX

Even matchsticks couldn't have kept my eyes open by the time I finally succumbed to sleep. Trepidation filled me in the moments of dreamless sleep before the dreamscape appeared. Would I have to face Dub and Carmen again in my dreams? Surely Killian would have warned me if they'd be able to harm me. What if I wasn't even able to make it to the dreamscape without my magic?

When the familiar meadow appeared around me, I blinked in confusion. It was the same as it had always been. The same soft grass beneath me, the same sun warming my skin. But something felt different.

Slowly, I stood and looked around, trying to put my finger on what it was that seemed off. It was a moment before I realised there was no sound. Where normally the dreamscape was vibrant with the symphony of nature, now it was just silent.

Unease slithered through me and I wrapped my

arms around myself, shivering despite the heat of the sun on my bare arms.

Killian would be here soon. There'd be a simple explanation; everything was fine.

I sat back down to wait.

<<<<<>>>>>

Who will Claim the magic? Find out in The Guardian's Truth

GET YOUR COPY
https://books2read.com/theguardianstruth

NOTE FROM THE AUTHOR

Thank you for joining me on this adventure through Ireland's hidden (for now) supernatural world. This is entirely a work of fiction, so while I have taken inspiration from well known Celtic myths, I hope you'll allow me some poetic license with these as I build this new and exciting world.

If you enjoyed this book, I would be very grateful if you could leave a brief review (it can be as short as you like) on the site where you purchased your copy.

As an author, reviews are the most powerful tools in my arsenal when it comes to getting attention for my books. Honest feedback goes a long way in increasing visibility and helping me to reach other readers like you, so thank you in advance!

*To get exclusive bonus material and be the first to hear about new releases, promotions, and giveaways **Sign up for my Newsletter at https://lmhatchell.com***

ALSO BY L.M. HATCHELL

To see the latest on all my books and upcoming publications, visit

https://lmhatchell.com/books